The Urbana Free Library

To renew: call 217-367-4057
or go to "*urbanafreelibrary.org*"
and select "Renew/Request Items"

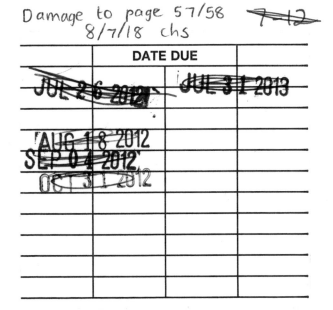

Damage to page 57/58   7-12
8/7/18 chs

	DATE DUE	
JUL 2 6 2012	JUL 3 1 2013	
AUG 1 8 2012		
SEP 0 4 2012		
OCT 3 1 2012		

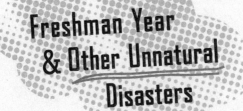

Freshman Year
& Other Unnatural
Disasters

Freshman Year & Other Unnatural Disasters

meredith zeitlin

G. P. PUTNAM'S SONS
An imprint of Penguin Group (USA) Inc.

7/12
17.00

G. P. PUTNAM'S SONS
A division of Penguin Young Readers Group.
Published by The Penguin Group.
Penguin Group (USA) Inc., 375 Hudson Street, New York, NY 10014, U.S.A.
Penguin Group (Canada), 90 Eglinton Avenue East, Suite 700, Toronto,
Ontario M4P 2Y3, Canada (a division of Pearson Penguin Canada Inc.).
Penguin Books Ltd, 80 Strand, London WC2R 0RL, England.
Penguin Ireland, 25 St. Stephen's Green, Dublin 2, Ireland
(a division of Penguin Books Ltd.).
Penguin Group (Australia), 250 Camberwell Road, Camberwell, Victoria 3124,
Australia (a division of Pearson Australia Group Pty Ltd).
Penguin Books India Pvt Ltd, 11 Community Centre,
Panchsheel Park, New Delhi—110 017, India.
Penguin Group (NZ), 67 Apollo Drive, Rosedale, Auckland 0632,
New Zealand (a division of Pearson New Zealand Ltd).
Penguin Books (South Africa) (Pty) Ltd, 24 Sturdee Avenue,
Rosebank, Johannesburg 2196, South Africa.
Penguin Books Ltd, Registered Offices: 80 Strand, London WC2R 0RL, England.

Design by Annie Ericsson. Text set in Meridien.

Library of Congress Cataloging-in-Publication Data
Zeitlin, Meredith.
Freshman year & other unnatural disasters / Meredith Zeitlin.
p. cm.
Summary: Smart, occasionally insecure, and ambitious Brooklyn fourteen-year-old Kelsey
Finkelstein embarks on her freshman year of high school in Manhattan with the intention
of "rebranding" herself, but unfortunately everything she tries to do is a total disaster.
[1. Self-acceptance—Fiction. 2. Self-perception—Fiction. 3. Friendship—Fiction.
4. Family life—New York (State)—New York—Fiction. 5. High schools—Fiction.
6. Schools—Fiction. 7. New York (N.Y.)—Fiction. 8. Humorous stories.]
I. Title. II. Title: Freshman year and other unnatural disasters.
PZ7.Z395Fr 2012 [Fic]—dc22 2011005690

ISBN 978-0-399-25423-9
1 3 5 7 9 10 8 6 4 2

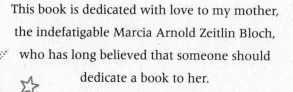

This book is dedicated with love to my mother,
the indefatigable Marcia Arnold Zeitlin Bloch,
who has long believed that someone should
dedicate a book to her.

And to my splendid sister, Joanna,
who is a one-eyed pirate.

1

Here it is, practically mid-September, and it's *still* too hot to live. I'm in the den trying to find anything worth watching on TV (fat chance on a Sunday night), and I can feel myself melting all over the couch. I love how my parents spend a million dollars putting in central air and then don't want to use it because it's "technically fall." Everyone in the tristate area is wearing shorts, and my delusional parents seem to think a cold front is going to hit Brooklyn in the next five minutes. Um, global warming, anyone?

My three best friends—Em, JoJo, and Cassidy—are on their way over here right now, so all I can do is hope that they're prepared for the Sahara-like conditions. Of course, they've been to my house about a zillion times, so they're familiar with the endless cycle of injustice that is my life.

I give up on the TV and head upstairs to the kitchen to get some snacks ready—and to make sure I'm closest to the front door. That way I can guarantee that my friends aren't intercepted by any nosy family members. Tonight is the last time we're all getting together before the first day of school on Tuesday, and I can't risk letting our important strategy session get sidetracked by my dad wanting to know if Em's dad is free for a thrilling racquetball game next Saturday, or my mother telling Cassidy she just *loves* her new earrings and had some just like them when she was our age and who wants to see pictures of her back in the glory days?!

Seriously, the things I deal with.

Em and Cassidy arrive just as I'm fishing a giant bag of Twizzlers from the back of a cupboard. They toss their overnight bags on the floor in the kitchen and pull up stools at the breakfast counter. "I thought you guys were meeting JoJo at the train," I say.

"We were," Cass explains, ripping into the Twizzlers with relish. "She texted that she was—"

"Running late?" I chime in simultaneously. JoJo is *always* running late.

"Yep." Em grins. She gets a can of root beer out of the fridge and takes a long sip. "Maybe it's time to give up on her. I mean, we've only been friends for a decade. Maybe enough is enough?"

It always amazes me how Em is sarcastic and silly around us but so sweet and shy at school. I wish more people got to see this side of her—but of course, she's been my very best friend since nursery school, so I know her better than anyone.

Cass adds, "Maybe we should start telling her we're meeting half an hour before we really are so she'll show up on time." She grabs a handful of Wheat Thins from a box on the counter. "Think that would work?"

"You guys have so little faith in me!"

JoJo suddenly appears in the door frame. Her hair has new turquoise streaks in it, which means she's been hanging out with her dad today. He was a guitarist with a semifamous band when he was young and refuses to let go of the dream. He has a Mohawk and lots of tattoos and is always encouraging JoJo to express herself. And he doesn't believe in rules, which works out great for the four of us when we go to her house.

Of course, right now we're at *my* house, and my mother absolutely cannot resist putting in an appearance. "Hi, girls! Eating us out of house and home for a change, I see?"

Ugggghhh. "Mom! Can you not?"

"Kelsey, have you been fiddling with the downstairs television set again? We put those parental controls on there for a reason, and it's a pain in the neck to keep resetting them all the time."

"I was just trying to—"

"Ooh, I like the new hair, JoJo. Very hip. And Em, I hear you had quite the romance at summer camp this year—I want to hear all about the lucky guy!"

As usual, the woman is unstoppable in her efforts to

embarrass me in front of my friends. I start scooping up our snacks, saying, "Mom, we'd love to chat, but we have a lot to do tonight, so we'll just relocate upstairs, if you don't mind. . . ." The girls and I start heading for the stairs.

"Big day on Tuesday, huh?" she calls, following us. "I know, I know, you don't want to talk to your horrible mother. Tell me, do you girls treat *your* mothers like this?"

I herd my friends into my room and close the door, but not before we hear: "No, that's fine, just ignore me—I'm used to the Typical Adolescent Behavior around here!"

She is seriously more annoying than any other person on the planet, including my dad. "Sorry, guys—you know how she is," I groan, flopping onto the floor.

"Yeah, exactly like everyone's mom. Except JoJo's," Cass points out. "And mine, obviously. But that's because I only see her, like, once a year."

Cass's mom decided one day that she felt like living in Paris and left, so now Cass lives with her dad and older brother a few blocks from me in Park Slope, Brooklyn. Some people have all the luck, I tell you.

"Twizzler, please!" JoJo sings, holding out a hand. Em passes her a fistful. "Thanks. I'd've gotten them myself, but I'm working on my Typical Adolescent Behavior."

"You didn't really tell her about James, did you?" Em asks me. James is the guy Em has been dating from camp for the last two months.

"Em, are you crazy?" I gasp. "Of course not! She sneakily read one of your letters—I left it on the kitchen table for about eight seconds, and by the time I got back it was too late. She's like the Secret Service."

"Hey, I know!" JoJo says, pausing to swallow a mouthful of licorice. "Let's spend all night talking about Kelsey's mom. Oooor . . . we could talk about Tuesday."

"Seriously. You only get one first day of high school, guys," adds Cass. "What's the plan?"

"Um, not get lost?" Em suggests. Em is brilliant, but she has the world's worst sense of direction.

"Not get expelled?" JoJo offers.

"Wow, we're really setting our sights on glory here," I say. "Way to aim high, you guys."

"Well, what did you have in mind, Kels? Like, streak through the cafeteria?"

"Yeah, Cass. That's it exactly—I thought we could streak through the caf."

I roll my eyes at her and she shrugs. "Well, just let me know what day so I can be sure to shave my legs."

I'll say this for Cass—she may be a little slow to catch up sometimes, but no matter what any of the three of us wants or needs, she's behind us one hundred percent. Of course, as our resident drama queen, she'd probably love the attention we'd get if we *did* streak the caf.

Cassidy grabs the Wheat Thins and lies down with her back on the floor and her legs straight up against the wall. It's part of a theater exercise or something—she's been doing it since she started taking acting classes in sixth grade. I'm used to it by now, but it's always fascinating to watch her eat upside down. And gross.

JoJo gives me a raised eyebrow. "What's going on, Kels? You have some big plan in mind or something?"

"No, not really. Just . . . well, we're in high school now. Obviously. And . . . it's time to defy expectations! To . . . change people's perceptions of us! I mean, I just feel like this year could be—"

"High school is still *school*, you know," JoJo scoffs. "Lame, unlikely to result in anything useful, and—"

"*Anyway*, I've decided to really . . . *do* something this year. To make a mark. Stand out. Revamp myself for a new era. You know, like Lady Gaga."

"You want to start wearing wigs and plastic bodysuits?"

"What? No. Okay—better example: Joan of Arc. You know, she wouldn't settle for the expec—"

"Wasn't she burned at the stake?!"

I sigh. "You're killing me, Cass."

"I'm just trying to understand what you mean!" She frowns.

"We might be here all night, then," JoJo says.

Cassidy sits up and swats her playfully on the arm. "Seriously, though, what are you going to do to make your big mark?"

"Well . . . I was thinking I'd start with soccer. I mean,

really take it seriously this year, work out on my own time . . ."

JoJo grins. "Hmm . . . I think I see where this is going now. Isn't there a certain star of the guys' soccer team that would be awfully impressed by that? Who could it be . . . ?"

Okay. It *is* true that Jordan Rothman, on whom I have had the world's biggest crush since approximately birth, is an amazing soccer player—he'll definitely make varsity, even as a freshman. And it's also true that guys who play soccer tend to hang out with girls who play soccer. But that is *not* the reason I decided to go in this direction. Come on— I'm not *that* pathetic.

Seriously.

Seriously!

"JoJo, playing soccer happens to be very important to me, and it has nothing to do with Jordan. I want to make JV and play left wing. And I'm going to do it!"

"I'm going to get a lead in the spring musical," Cass announces, upside down again. "I just started with a new vocal coach and she's *amazing*."

"See? This is the attitude I'm talking about!"

Em adds, "I think we should all follow your example, Kels. A positive attitude can *make* good things happen! And no," she continues, cutting off a smirking JoJo, "I'm not just saying that because my mom made me read *The Secret for Teens*. Although . . . it wasn't actually that bad."

Cass and I exchange a look and try not to laugh. Em really is the cutest—especially when she gets all earnest and turns bright red, like she is now.

JoJo starts digging through her bag for the shirt she brought to sleep in. "I think if you want to play soccer, then play soccer. Wear your uniform to school every day and do push-ups in the hall or . . . whatever. But I think there's an issue with your big plan. Like, a big one."

Cass jumps in before I can say anything. "Geez, JoJo! Why don't you just kick her in the shins while you're at it?"

"Well, no offense to Kelsey, she's a good player, but come on." JoJo turns back to me. "You can't start as left wing, as much as I want you to, obviously. Aren't you forgetting something? Or should I say some*one*?"

I scowl at her. Of course I know exactly who JoJo is talking about, but I'm *trying* to be positive, for crying out loud.

"Nope," I say firmly. "I don't think I'm forgetting anything."

"Um, Jemma Bradley? The girl who has beaten you out of that position every year since fourth grade?"

"And, also, well . . . you know. Jordan's girlfriend for the last three years," Em adds softly.

I squash a perfectly good mini Three Musketeers in frustration. Even *thinking* about Jemma Bradley—the most popular, prettiest, and nastiest girl in our grade—makes me crazy. But I'm determined not to let her ruin my year.

"This is a whole new ball game, ladies. The days of

Jemma lording it over everyone are *over*. I can feel it! I *will* be chosen for left wing this year, and she will be . . . well, maybe she'll decide to play field hockey instead. And we are not discussing Jordan, so don't even start," I add, sensing JoJo is about to reintroduce the subject of my lifelong obsession with one J. Rothman.

"Fine, fine, you win," she concedes. "I will try to fight my cynical nature for one evening, okay? So, what's everyone wearing on—"

Suddenly my bedroom door is flung wide open, and there's my nine-year-old sister, Travis. She's clutching the revolting blanky she should've been forced to throw away when she was four, and smirking. Very suspicious.

"Um, hello? Adults only. Go back to bed," I tell her.

She says, "I'm not going to bed—it's only nine o'clock! Besides, you aren't an adult. Get real."

Do you see how the little monster talks to me?!

"Trav, I loooove your pj's," Cass coos. She actually thinks Travis is cute, for some reason. "You look *so* adorable! Want a Twizzler?" Oh, lord. My sister is like a spaniel—once you feed her, she'll never leave. Thanks, Cassidy.

Travis stands there munching on the Twizzler, getting strawberry spit all over her hand. *Blech*. I'm just about to throw up in my own lap when she wipes her mouth with the already filthy blanky and chirps, "Hey, Kelsey?"

"What?"

"Guess what?"

"What?" This is ridiculous. Doesn't she understand that I have *company*?

"Remember that time when Mom brought me to visit you at camp?" She snags another Twizzler and a mini Snickers, too. Unbelievable.

"Uh, no? Can you go to bed now, please? Or go bug Mom or something?"

"Remember we watched your soccer game and you tripped over your own foot and your team lost?"

"Travis! Stop eavesdropping! Have you ever heard of privacy?"

"Whatever. You *suck* at soccer!" she yells, sticking out her tongue. I lunge in her direction, but she's gone, leaving only a crumpled wrapper in her wake.

The girls are unsuccessfully smothering their laughter.

"That isn't the whole story, you know. You've all seen me play! I should not have to defend myself against the ravings of a bratty little . . . Besides, that was two years ago. And we would've lost anyway, because this one girl kept shooting in the wrong goal and—aaaauuuugh!" Now I'm laughing, too.

We spend the rest of the night sifting through my wardrobe, which, as it turns out, is almost completely useless. I'd be lying if I said there aren't a few prank calls that get made—reining in JoJo Andover is not a task for the faint of heart, or even her best friends. All in all, it's a great night with my three favorite people in the world . . . even if I'm not completely sure they totally get my "defying expectations" idea.

I'll just have to *show* them what a great year this is going to be. Along with everyone else.

2

The next morning, after a breakfast of all the cereals in the house mixed together, my friends head out into the wide world of Park Slope. I am left at the kitchen table with Travis, who is picking all the marshmallows out of the Lucky Charms I had to trick my dad into buying by enthusiastically pointing out the "Whole Grains!" sticker on the box.

"Travis!" I snap. "Don't steal all the marshmallows and leave me the cereal part!"

She gives me her wide-eyed little sister look, complete with quivering lower lip. I sense a dramatic performance coming on, and since my parents are in the next room, I swiftly change the subject.

"Hey, Trav," I say conspiratorially, scooting my chair closer to hers. "Want Mom to take us shopping? I bet there's some stuff you need to start off the fourth grade in style, right? I mean, it's very important to look cool."

Travis looks at me suspiciously. "You just want Mom to take *you* shopping and you want *me* to ask her because I'm cute and adorable. Right?"

I tell you, this kid is impossible to trick. Or live with, for that matter.

"Well, sorry if I thought it would be nice for us to do something sisterly together, like getting ready for the first day of school. Forget it," I say, taking my empty bowl to the sink to rinse it. I throw in a disappointed sigh-sniff combo as I load it into the dishwasher.

Two can play this game.

Twenty minutes later, we're in the car. My mom (who hates lugging shopping bags on the subway and always insists on driving) heads into Manhattan, chattering the whole way about how nice it is that her girls are doing something as a team. Travis and I exchange pinches in the backseat. When, oh, when will my parents realize I should just be given a credit card and the autonomy to shop on my own? I'm in high school, for crying out loud. Has no one in this house besides me seen an episode of *Gossip Girl*?

My mom slows as we pass the SoHo Bloomingdale's and I start to feel a glimmer of hope. But then she keeps driving. When we get to Sixteenth Street, she hollers, "Girls—stop fooling around back there and look for an open meter!" and I suddenly realize where we're going.

The dreaded Loehmann's.

If you don't know, Loehmann's is this giant department store on Seventh Avenue that sells designer clothes at bargain prices. It is filled with old ladies who pick through the racks like vultures and fight over sequined scarves and scary pants with pleats all over them. If you're ever interested in seeing a teenager being forced to try on an appalling pom-pom-covered sweater against her will, you should definitely check it out.

The worst thing about Loehmann's is the communal dressing rooms—what sick person thought of that? I cannot accurately describe the creepiness of huddling in front of wall-to-wall mirrors, being forced to try on dorky jeans that I would *never* wear in public, while random strangers in giant granny panties look at me. Then my mother will inevitably shriek something like, "Oh, Kelsey, this blazer is so hip and in! Reese Witherspoon was wearing one just like it on the cover of *Glamour*! Just try it on to humor me, okay?"

Years from now, when my mother complains because I don't visit her in the nursing home, I will cite the Loehmann's dressing room as the reason. And she will see that she brought it all on herself.

After three migraine-inducing hours, during which Travis gets seven hundred things (clothes for little kids are pretty much the same no matter where you go), I end up with a pair of weird checked pants and a terrifying red blazer that are apparently "just perfect for the Jewish holidays!"

Obviously I was coerced into buying these items—I'm using what energy I have left to score a trip around the corner to Urban Outfitters, where maybe I can get *something* normal. And in a totally unsurprising turn of events, my request is summarily *denied*. Additionally, my lack of appreciation is pointed out repeatedly all the way home.

So here's the bottom line: I can either wear jeans and a shirt to the first day of school tomorrow, which I guess is fine but not really in keeping with my whole "taking charge of a new era" thing, or I can wear a shiny red blazer with my mom's horrifying dragonfly lapel pin on it. Tough choice, I know.

Did I mention I can feel a massive pimple waiting to spring to the surface directly under my nose? I bet it'll pop up like a crazy Hitler mustache the second I walk through the front doors of school, and I won't even realize it till someone *Sieg Heils* me.

Oh, God. It's going to be a disaster. I'm starting to totally freak out.

After dinner and a couple of hours spent trying on everything I own (again) and examining my upper lip area in my mom's magnifying mirror to see if the zit is any bigger yet, I go to my room and call Em. She says I should put toothpaste on it, which I immediately do. Can't hurt, right?

Then she asks, "Kels? Is there anything bothering you? Don't get me wrong—I'm totally behind your soccer stuff and anything else you want to do. I just . . . well, you don't have to prove anything to anybody, you know? Everyone likes you the way you are. I just want to make sure you know that."

Oh, Em. What would I do without her? "You're so sweet

to say that, and no, nothing is bothering me," I say. "Well, not really. It's just . . . I guess I feel like high school is a chance to . . . I don't know. I feel like, finally, it's my turn to . . . something. You know what I mean?"

"Oh, yeah. That totally clears it up."

I laugh. "I'm just trying to figure out what my place is going to be. Maybe I watched too much *Oprah* this summer or something, but I feel like it's my chance to . . . be . . . I mean, why should evil Jemma Bradley always get everything she wants, especially when she's such a . . . ? Well, anyway, I'm always going to be the same delightful Kelsey you love and adore, and you'll still have to hang out with me, so don't get any ideas."

Em groans. "Damn. Here I thought this was my chance to get rid of you for good."

"Sorry. Your plans have been foiled. So, have you talked to James? Think he'll come to visit?"

Em launches into a hundred-miles-a-minute recap about her latest Skype conversation with James. I'm totally listening, but all my thoughts about school tomorrow are still buzzing around in the back of my brain. I feel like I'm on the cusp of something—that maybe in a new place, with new people, I can be the best version of myself. Explore the possibilities that maybe I didn't take seriously enough in stupid middle school.

". . . and then he said that his parents probably wouldn't let him visit at Thanksgiving because obviously they want him to be with *them*, and my parents would never let me go to his house because they're like 'blah blah, you're only fourteen, it's not as if you're going to marry this boy, you'll get over it,' which is so beyond insulting—"

"Em, your parents are being ridiculous. Who's thinking about getting married, for crying out loud?"

That's another thing. Guys. How did it happen that I'm the only one of my friends—including Em, the shy one!—who has never hooked up with anyone? Not that I haven't had any chances, mind you. A certain Keith Mayhew has been frantically pursuing me since sixth grade. (He's totally nice, but . . . I don't like him *that* way.) I just want my first real kissing experience to be this utterly awesome thing, with the right guy and the right situation. And I know fourteen isn't *that* old . . . but it feels like I've totally missed the boat. I mean, I am seriously the only one now. And what if my friends start having sex or something before I even get to first base, and I'm still wandering around, unkissed, unnoticed? I'll just die of humiliation. Not that I can imagine anyone (especially myself) having sex with any of the guys I know—or anything leading up to sex, really. It all seems so awkward and sort of gross . . . and yet it's what I think about ALL THE TIME.

Maybe I'm going crazy? This is why I should focus on the soccer tryouts. Left wing, left wing . . .

". . . which makes me really nervous because, I mean, I've only known him for three months and he's been so sweet about taking things slow . . . but what if he has some kind of crazy hormonal surge and—"

Well, it's comforting to know that I'm not the only one thinking about this stuff, anyway.

I suddenly realize it's almost midnight, so Em and I say good night and I get ready for bed, trying not to look in the mirror for fear of what I might see there. Beauty-sleep time. Maybe the pimple-to-be will disappear during the night.

3

Sometime around dawn, my evil alarm clock goes off, and after five or six rounds of hitting the snooze button, I only have about twelve seconds to get out of the house. Awesome. At least the pimple decided not to make an appearance. Toothpaste. Who knew?

I quickly get dressed—and *not* in the heinous Loehmann's options. I'm in the kitchen scarfing down an English muffin when my mom comes in and starts rooting around in her briefcase.

She looks up and says, "So, your father and I agreed that we'll take you to school for the first couple of days to make sure you're comfortable on the subway. Get a move on—we have to leave in five minutes or I'll be late for work."

Um, excuse me, what? "Mom, I've only been taking the subway by myself *all summer*. Am I suddenly going to get kidnapped? I think not. So . . . thanks, but no thanks."

"This is not up for discussion, Kelsey. It's early, the station is crowded, you have a lot on your mind . . . God forbid something happens to you. Don't start with me."

"Mom, I'm in *high school,* remember? I'm not five years old! This is completely un—"

"Kelsey, if you don't like it, you can bang your head against the wall and spit wooden nickels."

That's one of her very favorite nonsensical sayings/conversation enders. Why she hasn't been carted off to the lunatic asylum yet is truly beyond me.

Five fury-filled minutes later, we all head out in a sullen Finkelstein parade. There's my dad on the right, clutching his travel thermos for dear life and shooting me winks, like, "Hey, Kelsey, let's just humor your ol' mom, okay?" To my left is my delightful mother, carrying a shopping bag along with her briefcase and purse, and sporadically saying things like, "On *my* first day of high school back in 1917, I wore a beautiful dress I made myself by the light of our one candle," and wiping my sister's nose for her, though when I was nine, I'm pretty sure I had mastered the art of using a tissue.

After twenty-five minutes of sitting on the F train to Manhattan (with me in a separate row of seats so the entire world won't immediately know that I'm with my parents), we finally get to Fourteenth Street. We drop Travis off at the elementary school building, at which point I try to say a swift good-bye to my parents and head over to the high school on my own. Fat chance— they follow right behind me. Thankfully, Em comes up at that exact moment and meets me by the side entrance like we planned. She looks as if she's about to burst with excitement.

"Oh my God, Kels, I'm so glad you're here. You will *never* believe the news!" she gushes. I haven't seen Em this excited since she told me about her first makeout session with James.

"What's going on? Tell me!"

"Jemma. Bradley. Moved. To. *Arizona*."

I just gape at her, disbelieving. Then we both forget to be extremely cool and age appropriate and start screeching and dancing around like lunatics. I just wish Cass and JoJo were with us to celebrate this glorious, glorious moment: Jemma Bradley is *gone*! Gone to live in the Arizona desert with only a cactus as a friend. Maybe she'll get chased by a pack of coyotes into some quicksand and never be heard from again!

"Isn't this amazing news?" Em shrieks. Even Em, who likes everybody, doesn't like Jemma.

"How did you find this out?" I demand.

"My dad works with Jemma's dad, you know, and my parents were talking about it at breakfast—I was going to call you but I wanted it to be a surprise."

This is unbelievable. Now we can all enjoy freshman year without wasting a single second worrying about accidentally pissing off an evil, blond-ringleted dictator with no sense of humor at all. Next thing you know, they'll be serving birthday cake for lunch every day.

Em and I grin at each other. "This is going to be the best year ever. I can feel it," I say.

"Me too!" Em agrees.

Suddenly my mother invades our happy-dance circle and clutches my arm. "Kels, I need to speak with you privately before you go zipping off into your new life. How about that bench over there?"

I immediately know that she is going to do something horrible, like kiss me in front of the free world or warn me about teenage pregnancy. Inevitably it will be something so embarrassing that I will have to throw myself down a well.

I heave an enormous sigh, tell Em to go ahead without me, and sit on the bench with my mom for our chat. Behind us, kids are heading inside, taking pictures, laughing, and generally not having chats with their mothers.

Mom takes my hand (seriously? In public?) and says, "You know, Kels, I really discovered myself in high school. Looking back, it was truly a crossroads between childhood and adulthood for me, and that's very important. Now that you're entering this phase of your life . . ."

This is even worse than I anticipated. Bring on the "just in case" condom to carry in my backpack.

". . . I know it's not easy to be fourteen, and I want you to *know* that I know. Okay?"

"Um . . . sure, Mom." *What do I say to this? Thanks?* "Thanks."

She looks at me and I look back. I can tell she's about to

do the thing where she silently beams at me for five minutes and then recounts the story of my birth—definitely no time for that today. I force a smile. "So . . . are we done? Because I don't want to be late for homeroom, so . . ."

"Okay, okay. Go in. But listen—I want you to be yourself. Let everyone know what a fabulous person you are and how much you have to offer. You really are terrific, you know that?"

Well, now I feel a little bad for wanting to throw myself down a well. "Thanks, Mom. Really." I smile for real this time.

She takes a small box out of her pocket and hands it to me. I open it . . . and there's a gift card to Urban Outfitters inside.

Every once in a rare while, my mom can be pretty cool.

"Mom, thanks! This is great!" I exclaim.

"Use it for whatever you want. Oh—that reminds me, speaking of clothes . . ."

I'm tucking the gift card into a pocket of my backpack when she pulls it out of the shopping bag: the scary red blazer that I purposely left on the chair in my room with the tags still on.

"You forgot this! I figured you'd need it in case it's chilly with the AC on," she says.

Is there a wicked glint in her eye, or is it my imagination?

"Uh . . . I think I'll be okay," I stammer, desperately

looking around for someone to signal to for help. "I should probably save that for temple, right?"

"Well, I think you're responsible enough to take care of it for one day. Put it on—I want to see you all dressed up in front of your new school."

She's basically shoving me into the jacket; I figure struggling is futile, so I shrug it on and plan to stash it in my locker ASAP.

And then, just as I'm fully encased in blazery ugliness and Mom is tugging at my sleeves . . . Jordan Rothman walks by. Oh, God—he's even cuter than he was at the end of last year! His dirty blond hair is a little longer now and he keeps brushing it out of his eyes, which just happen to be the bluest on the *planet*. I swear, they're like lasers that just zap you the second he looks your way. I think he's definitely grown a couple of inches over the summer, too. He's with a bunch of guys from our grade, and there's just no contest—he is the hottest, sexiest, best-looking one there.

Swoon.

I come back down to earth and realize that I have to hide myself immediately before the blue lasers catch sight of my hideously updated ensemble.

"Mom, I *really* have to go. Thanks so much for the gift card, and—"

"Ooh, is that Jordan Rothman?" she whispers loudly. "He's turned into quite the hunk! I wonder if his mom still—"

I turn frantically and see Jordan snickering to his friends. Oh, God.

"I have to *go*, Mom! See you later, love you, bye!" I dash off as fast as I can before she can start talking to Jordan about his mother or anything else, pausing only when I almost trip over some guy taking pictures of his friends by the front door.

Well, that was an auspicious beginning.

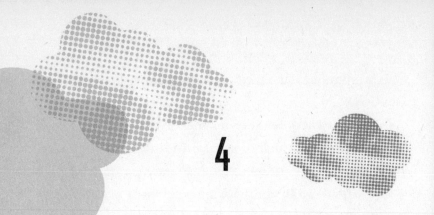

4

I've been in high school for three days now, and thus far it's been a complete and total suckfest. Were all the teachers at this school forbidden to watch TV or eat candy growing up? Why are they so mean? Have they made some kind of pact designed to torture innocent kids who just want to text each other during homeroom?

I can't believe how much more work there is compared to middle school. I mean, pop quizzes? Really? On the *second day of school*? And in what world is it okay for my econ teacher to *assign* us partners for a project instead of letting us choose our own? What happened to spending the first week getting to know each other and talking about our summers? And I got paired with, of all possible choices, Danny Zifner, who has smelled like old meat since third grade. What if it's contagious in close proximity? What if the whole year is like this and I have to do tons of work and it ruins *EVERYTHING*?

But right now, for the next few hours, I have soccer

tryouts—time to slap on my new positive attitude. Let the shining begin!

I quickly change clothes in the girls' locker room and head out to the field. The ground is nice and firm and it isn't too hot out—I'm feeling really good. We start with stretching, and in between toe touches I suss out the competition. Most of my middle-school teammates are here, of course, and a lot of girls I don't know at all—mainly upperclassmen, I guess. I recognize a couple of older girls who I know are the big varsity stars and make a mental note to try to end up in their group if we do a scrimmage.

The coaches assign some girls to set up cones for drills, and I join a bunch of friends from my old team in line. Ana Blau, who was one of our starting forwards in eighth grade, leans in and whispers, "I still can't believe Jemma is gone. You must be pretty psyched, huh?"

I smile at her and shrug.

Ana's best friend, Keri, says, "Well, *I'm* psyched. It'll be a nice change not to have to huddle under a sweatshirt in the locker room so she doesn't make fun of my boobs or whatever."

"Let's just say I think we will all have a splendid year and leave it at that," I say loftily. Keri and Ana laugh.

"You gonna go for left—"

"Pay attention!" a mean-looking girl (who has clearly never come into contact with a much-needed pair of tweezers) snaps at us. Yeesh. This isn't the army, for Pete's sake. Chill out.

A coach blows her whistle, so we shut up and get ready for drills. Passing to the other line down the field, sprinting and shooting on the goal, speed ladders . . . it's exhausting, but I'm so pumped up with adrenaline that I kind of coast along. I think the coach who's working with our group has noticed me, because she keeps putting me in the line with the faster runners each round. And I only missed once on goal, which is pretty good.

After about a thousand hours of drills, we get divided up into groups for scrimmages; Ana is on my team, which is great, because I know how she plays. We get our pinnies—disgusting yellow mesh vests that go on over our shirts—and line up. I'm playing right wing, which is fine. The important thing is to stand out. I desperately want to avoid getting stuck on third string, which is basically the team for everyone who didn't make JV. Usually all freshmen and maybe a sophomore or two.

Third string does *not* fit into my plan for the year.

We get the whistle to start, and the girl I'm guarding, Sara, is the fastest runner I've ever seen—I can barely keep up with her. Of course, she's also about six inches taller than I am, which definitely gives her an edge.

I decide to try a different strategy about halfway through the game and go way back toward my team's goal instead of chasing her. When the goalie blocks a shot, it goes flying right to me. I stop it with my knee, snag the ball, and just GO GO GO down the field on the opposite side. Yessssss!

I'm running like crazy and I just know Sara is on top of me but I pass to Ana and keep going and she crosses it back to me and I kick as hard as I can on an angle—YESSSSSSSSSSSS!!!! I accept high fives from my teammates as I jog off the field. There's no way the coach won't consider me for JV now. Maybe even varsity, which would be crazy incredible. I'm so psyched I can barely keep still, but Ana and Keri and I sit together to watch some of the other groups play. I'm pleased to note that Ms. Crazy Eyebrows is not very good—hopefully she'll end up on third string and I won't get stuck being snarled at by her for the rest of the season.

The following Monday, after a rousing debate in econ with Danny "Meat-Scented For Your Horror" Zifner over whether making a poster with colored markers is too juvenile (it is), I ditch my books and head with Em and Cass to the cafeteria for lunch. On the way, we see a crowd of kids around the bulletin board where they post notices and stuff, all looking very excited. Could they have posted team rosters already? The older kids started tryouts before the first day of school, so maybe . . .

All of a sudden I'm really nervous. What if the coach

didn't notice me at all? What if I *do* make JV but I'm the worst one on the team and instead of starting I end up on the bench all season, totally humiliated? What if—

"Let's go look!" Em says excitedly, and she and Cass start to shove me forward.

"Kels, this is your big moment! Get up there!" Cass exclaims. She and Em are giving me huge, encouraging smiles, so I take a deep breath, tell myself, *This is your year of greatness! Pull it together, Finkelstein!* and elbow up toward the board.

Field hockey, football, and tennis are up there, too, so the crowd is pretty intense. Luckily they list girls and guys separately or I'd probably get squashed by some overexcited linebacker. I'm almost to the board when I spot Ana in the front of the mob, giving me a thumbs-up. My heart leaps—does that mean she made it, or I did, or both? Or is she just doing weird thumb exercises that are totally unrelated to soccer? I push farther forward so I can finally see the list. I quickly skim the varsity team—all junior and senior names from what I can tell. No surprises there. On to junior varsity . . .

I MADE IT!

I'm so relieved, I almost forget I'm in the middle of a surging crowd of kids, some of whom are looking decidedly pissed off. I'm leaning in for a second look to see which of my friends also made JV—and who didn't—when, right beside me, I hear, "It's total BS, doll. I mean, obviously you deserved to make varsity this year. The coach is a moron."

I turn to look and it's this theater guy that I recognize from pictures of plays hanging in the hallway. He's got to be a junior or a senior, and he's wearing a lot of guyliner and all black clothes. And he's talking to the obnoxious girl with the eyebrow wigs from tryouts.

Crap. Does this mean she's on JV with me?

"Do you *mind*?" she snaps now, breaking my train of thought. "I'm *trying* to get to my locker!" Before I can even respond, she pushes past me.

Well, I guess I know whom to root for to win MVP at the sports assembly this year.

I wend my way back to Cass and Em, who can tell by my face that I made the team, and we all take a second to flail around with excitement. Then we remember that as freshmen we should call as little attention to ourselves as possible, and slink off to the cafeteria to meet JoJo.

As I'm clutching my tray (carrot and raisin salad as a side? Really?) and scanning the tables for available seats, I see Ana and Keri waving us over. Ana made JV, too, which is so fantastic. Unfortunately, Keri got on third string. Not that it's the end of the world—we're only lowly frosh, after all—but I know how disappointed I would have been, so we do our best to cheer her up.

I'm telling them about my exchange at the bulletin board, scanning the room till I can point out drama guy and our new super-friendly teammate. Ana says, "Oh, her. Yeah, that's Julie Nelson. She sucks, but she's a junior, which is the only reason she got on JV at all."

"She looks scary," Keri adds, smiling for the first time. "And if she's a junior, she'll probably end up being captain. Good luck, you guys."

"She's in my Spanish class and she *is* scary," Cass informs us. "Also terrible at Spanish, obviously. But she's really popular. I heard her parents are loaded and she has these big parties, so everyone basically worships her even though she's a jerk."

"Ah, the mysteries of pseudo-adulthood . . . ," JoJo says, biting into something unidentifiable on her tray.

"So now what? She hates me!" I groan.

"Say something friendly to her," Em suggests. "You know, be casual but nice. Look—she's back in line, so go get a soda or something and say hi."

This seems a bit pathetic, but I figure it's worth a shot. Everyone in the world likes Em, so I trust her advice. I get up and join the line, and when Julie is walking past me, I touch her arm to get her attention.

She whips around like I burned her, glaring. She's at least five inches taller than I am and has huge linebacker shoulders. Everything she's wearing is straight out of a magazine, and she's got a Prada purse slung over her shoulder, which makes her frizzy hair and ungroomed eyebrows even more baffling—you'd think she'd have a stylist or something.

Maybe she's afraid of waxing? Speaking of the eyebrows, they look even bushier than they did before. What if they leap off her face and attack me? Yipes.

"Oh, hey, Julie, uh, I'm Kelsey," I stutter. "Just wanted to say, um, I'm really psyched that you're on my soccer team, and—"

She stares at me like I just murdered her whole family and growls, "Oh, I didn't realize it was *your* soccer team. I'll be sure to keep that in mind, *freshman*."

Then she stomps off, probably to tell the whole school about the conversation and make everyone think I'm some kind of stuck-up jerk. What the eff? I slide back in next to JoJo at our table and she goes, "Well, that looked like a successful chat. Do you want your carrot salad, by the way?"

I hand over the disgusting salad. "I just said it was cool we're both on JV and she had a total attack or something. What is her problem? And what do I do *now*—any more helpful suggestions? Anyone?"

I look across the caf and notice Julie talking feverishly to her tablemates and pointing in my direction. Em squeezes my arm. "Maybe she just got dumped and is feeling extra sensitive."

"Who would date her?" JoJo asks through a mouthful of shredded carrot. "She wears too much makeup. And so does her pal Ned, for that matter."

"What? Who's Ned?" I ask.

"The guy next to her in all black, Ned Garman. He's, like,

the big drama guy in the senior class," Cass gushes. "I can't *wait* to be in a show with him. He takes acting classes at—"

"Oh, *that* guy. Right." I take a bite of my lunch. Bad idea. "Seems weird that a Park Avenue princess is hanging out with a Gothy theater dude, though, doesn't it?"

"Oh, they've been best friends forever. He's loaded, too—just trying to piss off his parents, probably," Keri says.

I glance back toward Julie's table. Ned is laughing hysterically at what Julie is saying and waving his hands around like a loon. "Great. He's probably got an even bigger mouth than Julie does. Now I'm gonna have to be on damage control for the rest of the day and, possibly, my life."

"Probably she just feels bad about being one of the only juniors on JV and thought you were rubbing it in," Em reassures me. "I'm sure she'll forget all about it."

Cass jerks her head in Julie's direction. "Or . . . maybe not."

Julie has gotten up and passes by our table with some friends in tow, including Ned. Julie sneers, "See you at *your* practice, Kelsey. Thanks so very much for letting me attend."

I feel like putting my head in a vat of tar and leaving it there forever. But I'm going to have to make the best of it. I mean, I set a goal for myself (no pun intended) and I'm not going to let some bitter junior with a grooming problem screw it all up for me. I will soldier on! I can overcome this hurdle!

"Hey, Kels," JoJo says, interrupting my inner pep talk. "Uh, is this you?"

She holds up a copy of *The Reflector,* our school newspaper. On the front page is an article about the first day of the new school year. Under the headline is a picture of a bunch of kids posing with their arms around each other in front of the main building.

What is JoJo talking about? I never—

Oh, no.

In the background of the picture, sort of lurching toward the door, is a girl. A girl who certainly bears a resemblance to me. A girl who is wearing a horrible blazer resplendent with a dragonfly pin. The same blazer that is now in a ball at the bottom of my locker.

"Yep. That's me, all right," I finally admit.

"Well, you wanted to be noticed." JoJo is clearly trying very hard not to laugh. "It's only the second week of school and you already made the front page!"

5

Em spent the rest of that week insisting that no one else would ever notice me in the background of the picture and that I shouldn't worry about it. I personally found it hard to believe that a photo of a girl with gravity-defying bangs whose mouth is hanging open—not to mention sporting the fashion statement of the year, of course—wouldn't attract some interest, but she was right. (Unless you count JoJo and Cass, who both have copies in their binders for easy reference and dissolve into hysterical laughter every time one or the other brings it up. Hardy har har.) Of course, I *did* consider hunting down the kid who took the picture and initiating a discussion on the journalistic ethics of candid photography, but since it's credited simply to STAFF PHOTOGRAPHER, that seems like a lot of investigative work and I just don't have the energy.

Week three of my high school career starts off with my mother harassing me all through breakfast. "So, Kels—let's dish! Who are you hanging out with at lunch? What's up with Em and the other girls? Any new boys in your classes? How about that cutie Jordan, hmmm? Did you decorate your locker this year or is that 'so eighth grade'? If I keep asking you these annoying questions, are you going to pull out your eyeballs and hurl them at the ceiling?!"

I don't know why she has this insatiable need to know everything about my life. I wish she'd just eat her toast and reminisce to *herself* about her own high school experience (which apparently revolved around thinking Matthew Broderick was cool and having the world's most terrifying shoulder-pad collection) and leave me alone. I'm starting to understand why breakfast bars were invented—so you can eat and run away from annoying parents at the same time.

I escape to school and manage to stay awake until 3:15. Then I head to my first official JV soccer practice. As I approach the field, I send up a silent prayer: *Please, please let Julie Nelson have forgotten all about me so I can get back to being psyched about the team and having a killer season. And let me get picked to start. As left wing. Please?*

The other girls and I spread out on the field, stretching, lacing up cleats, and catching up on the gossip from the weekend. Our coach, Ms. Cantwell, comes over, tapping on her clipboard.

"Okay, girls," she grunts. "Welcome, congratulations, et cetera. Let's get to work."

We all go to grab a ball from the big bags and start warming up. I do my best to avoid Julie Nelson's evil eye.

After a while, the coach calls us back in and we sit on the grass. "Is everyone drinking enough water?" she asks. We nod. "Good. That's important. Now, let's go ahead and pick a team captain. Responsibilities include assisting me, posting game schedules, blah blah blah . . ."

I exchange a look with Ana. We know what's coming next. Some girl raises her hand like she heard they're giving away free money and practically shouts, "I nominate Julie!" Ana rolls her eyes at me, and I almost laugh, but since I'm trying to be on my best behavior, I manage to hold it in.

The team takes a vote; every single person votes for Julie, including me. I feel like I've helped seal my own coffin, but I would definitely make things worse by being the only person *not* voting for her. So I'm hoping she will see the proverbial white flag I've waved and let bygones be bygones.

Julie jumps up and starts making an acceptance speech like she just won an Oscar or something. As I'm thinking about what homework I have to do tonight, I notice a blond girl jogging over to our group from across the field. I've never seen her before, and believe me—I'd remember her.

You know those moments in movies when the gorgeous

babe walks past a pool or something and a song comes on and everything suddenly goes into slow motion? This girl could be in that moment. She must be in high school since she's here, but she could easily pass for at least twenty-two. She looks like a model: perfect, delicate features, long blond hair, and a tiny diamond in her right nostril. Her legs are about as long as my entire body, and she's smiling like someone just told her she won the "World's Whitest Teeth" contest.

She saunters over to Coach Cantwell and they have a short conversation. Julie is still droning on about how terrific she'll be as captain when Cantwell interrupts her.

"Okay, girls—this is Lexi Bradley. She's a freshman like some of you and just moved here from Los Angeles. Now, she's gonna be on JV with us even though she missed try-outs; she was All-American at her junior high school. Make her feel welcome!"

Wait a sec. Did Cantwell say Lexi *BRADLEY*? As in *Jemma* Bradley?!

Surely it's a coincidence.

"All right, count off for scrimmage!" the coach hollers, and Julie is suddenly looming into my field of vision.

"Snap out of it, freshman! Don't want *your* team starting without you, do you?" she sneers. Well, great. So much for the proverbial white flag.

As I scramble to my feet, I overhear Lexi saying, "Yeah, she's my cousin. I guess it's kind of like I'm taking her place, right?"

Cue adorable giggle.

WHYYYYYYYYYYYYYYYY?!

6

It only takes a single day for me to realize that Lexi is way too busy being admired to even notice me shooting her death-ray looks across every hallway and classroom. She has a lot on her plate, after all, what with crossing and uncrossing her endless legs in their $250 jeans, giggling, and flipping her perfect, evil, cascading blond locks.

Not that I'm spending all my time watching Lexi. Most of the time I watch Jordan Rothman watching her. Day by day, my meticulously imagined future with him slips away from me like a helium balloon on a windy day.

At lunch on Wednesday, Em says to me, "Kels, you should give Lexi a chance. I mean, she's in my math class and she's actually *really* nice. Besides, you don't know that Jordan is interested in her. Or that she even likes *him*! Maybe he's just trying to figure out the best way to ask you out and it's taking a while to, you know . . ."

"Well, Kels, you'd better get in there," JoJo interrupts. "Lexi is *hot*."

Cass, Em, and I exchange a look around the table. JoJo looks up from her hummus and avocado sandwich when we don't say anything. "What? Well, she is."

"She is definitely hot," I agree. "It just doesn't seem *fair*. No one our age should look that good! I bet she's a narc."

I will admit (reluctantly) that Lexi really *is* a good soccer player, so she didn't get on the team just for being gorgeous and popular. And she's a forward, so at least I've kept my position—for now. I'm still hoping I'll get to be in the starting lineup, but with the first game coming up in no time at all, you never know what could happen.

As we leave the caf, Em and JoJo are walking ahead of me and Cassidy. I lean toward Cass and whisper, "Should we just ask JoJo if she's into girls? I mean, she's so open about everything usually . . . it's freaking me out that she hasn't talked to us about this at *all*."

Cass whispers back, "Maybe she's testing us to see what we'll say or something?" She shrugs. "I dunno, Kels. Maybe she isn't sure yet? I don't want to make her feel pressured to, like, come out or something, you know? But then she talks about how hot some girl is and I don't know what to say! Maybe we *should* ask her? But what if she isn't and then we make her feel weird because we thought . . . ugh. I don't know."

I feel bad talking behind JoJo's back—literally—but I really want to figure this thing out. The three of us have been having the same conversation for months now, but we haven't actually said anything because we don't want to screw it up and make JoJo feel uncomfortable. I mean, JoJo is our *bestie*. She could talk to us about anything and we'd be there for her, but she isn't talking to us about maybe being gay at *all*—except for the random comments. I hate thinking she's worried we won't understand or something . . . but like Cass said, I don't want to push her if she isn't ready.

"Me neither. So, better to wait, then, right? Oh—there's the bell." I wave to Em and JoJo and head down the hall to class.

On Friday, practice is canceled because of rain. The fields are a muddy mess, and the guys' team takes over the gym. I'm sort of hoping we get assigned to watch and cheer them on. Jordan face time is always a bonus, and I haven't exactly been hanging out with him this year as I planned (gazing at him longingly doesn't count), but Coach Cantwell tells us to take the day off.

I go to meet Em by her locker and am intercepted by Keith Mayhew, my number one fan. Since school started, he has displayed an uncanny ability to pop up whenever I'm by myself or to corner me after any class we have together. I guess it should be flattering . . . but it's actually kind of creepy.

It's not that there's anything so wrong with Keith—well, his eyes are sort of uneven. Okay, okay—I'm being shallow and ridiculous. Keith is nice and kind of funny and a good guy in general. Maybe it's because he's always been so obvious about liking me? No. It's more like . . . I dunno. He's no Jordan Rothman—let's leave it at that.

"Hey, Kels, where're you heading?" he starts, sidling up next to me. "It's really coming down out there, y'know? Hope you've got an umbrella. You want me to lend you one? I've got an extra in my locker, y'know, because my mom told me—"

"Thanks, Keith," I say, trying to be pleasant yet escape at the same time. "I'm actually meeting Em and she's got one, so I'm all set. But see you later!" I dash off and grab Em, who is waiting for me in front of her locker and texting James. We decide to detour to Antonio's Pizza, which is the unofficial after-school hangout.

Off we trudge through the pouring rain, both of us huddling under Em's giant golf umbrella and trying not to fall into any puddles. Of course, by the time we make it inside, I look like a drowned rat anyway.

I get a slice, fill up my cup with Dr Pepper, and look for a table. I spot Ana sitting with Lexi and some other girls from the team, and then Lexi calls out, "Hey, Kelsey! Over here!" and flashes her giant smile right at me.

This is sort of surprising, since I've said about three

words to her since she arrived. (None of which were the ones I *wanted* to say, namely, "Go back to where you came from, and take your evil Bradley-ness with you!") Maybe she's just excited because her beauty will be even further showcased by sitting next to me in my current incarnation as a mud creature?

Em gives me a look, like, *See? She's nice!*

Whatever.

As we dig in, Lexi asks, "Hey, Em, can you believe how much work Dr. Shanman gave us for Monday? Some of us have lives, you know?"

"I know—I was hoping to maybe visit my boyfriend this weekend," Em sighs, blushing on the word *boyfriend* as usual, "but I've got a paper and so much other stuff . . ."

"Oh, you were gonna visit James? That's awesome! I mean, sucks to cancel, but—"

Um, what? How does Lexi know about James? What is going on in this math class, exactly? I'm about to say something like, "So, have you made out with my future husband Jordan Rothman lately?" when I feel a sharp tap on my shoulder. I turn my head and am greeted by a horrible sight: Julie Nelson, looming in all her scariness directly above me.

"Hey, Julie, what's up?" I say, trying for nonchalance.

"Hey, guys," she greets the rest of the table. "I just need to borrow Kelsey for a sec, 'kay?"

I shoot Em a look of despair—*don't let me be borrowed by Julie Nelson!*—and push back my chair. Lexi continues yammering on about Em and James, which I guess makes sense. I mean, it's not like I can give Em any good advice about boys, seeing as the only ones I come into direct contact with are either unappealing (Zifner, Mayhew) or ignoring me (everyone else).

I trudge behind Julie to a table in the corner, sit down, and watch her blot pizza with a napkin for about a lifetime. My phone vibrates in my pocket, and I take it out to see a lovely text from my mother about dishes in the sink and how she's not my maid. *Thanks, Verizon,* I think, *for making your phones so user-friendly that even the elderly can send text messages.* I put the phone on the table and weigh the pros and cons of dramatically clearing my throat to get Julie's attention. (Cons win. I sit in silence, waiting.)

Finally, Julie glares at me haughtily and announces, "Well, Kelsey, I've got good news and bad news. The bad news is that Katie Stolting broke her ankle last night and she can't play for the rest of the season. But the good news is that I think you're the *perfect* person to replace her, especially since you're sooooo excited about *your* team and all. I suggested it to Coach Cantwell, and she said that it was absolutely the best possible idea."

She takes a huge bite of pizza, gulps it down, and looks at me with a nefarious gleam in her eye. "No need to thank me. Your obvious excitement is thanks enough." She smirks at me for a second, then her face hardens back into its usual glare. "You can go away now."

I sit there, still stunned. Julie growls, "I *said* go back to your little pals. *My* friends sit at this table, freshman."

I manage to push my chair back and stand up. I'm about two steps away from the table when she calls my name again. I turn back to see what else she could possibly have to add.

"I forgot to say congrats," Julie purrs, smiling spitefully, *"GOALIE."*

7

I continue my slow march back to my table. Katie's a junior, like Julie, and got stuck on the JV team because she's one of only three people who plays the position almost no one ever wants to play: goalie. And now I'm supposed to take over? How could Katie break her ankle at night in her own house, I'd like to know? Was she practicing Irish dancing on the stairs or something? Why is she such a klutz??

I suddenly realize that if I don't leave Antonio's immediately, I'm going to start crying. Which is so not like me, but I can feel a stinging behind my eyes and my throat starting to close up.

Em is looking at me across the pizzeria like, *What's going on?* I take a deep breath and go back to my original table to get my backpack. Lexi, who has somehow managed to eat all of her pizza without getting a single drop of grease or sauce on her white T-shirt, asks, "Kelsey, what happened? You look awful!"

Well, that certainly makes me feel less like crying. This just gets better and better.

I smile as best as I can and say, "Oh, you know, the dragon lady just needed someone to sharpen her claws on."

A few of the girls laugh, but Em looks concerned and starts to get up. "What happened? Do you want me to—"

"Yeah, I'm just gonna head out, so I'll talk to you guys later, okay?" Em can always tell when I want to be alone, and she sits back down. I grab my bag and walk as quickly as I can to the door. When I get outside, I start to run, because the tears are definitely coming. Of course it's not even drizzling anymore, so I can't let them out and pretend it's just rain. But I don't want anyone—especially Julie or Lexi—to see me cry over a stupid thing like being goalie.

This is the cruelest thing Julie could've done to me—force me to spend every game stuck inside the net, trying not to get smashed by goal shots whizzing toward me, cloaked in the stench of sweaty (and in this case, used) goalie armor. I don't know how to guard the goal! And forget reeling in Jordan Rothman or anyone else on the guys' team—they'll think I weigh three hundred pounds and have a sweat-gland disorder. I'll probably develop a chronic case of backne. Or have my face caved in by a rogue ball. Then I'll have to get complete reconstructive surgery, end up looking like Mickey Rourke, and no one will know I'm on the team at all.

Why does Julie hate me so much? Is this really all because of one stupid comment in the cafeteria when I was actually trying to be *nice*?

I run all the way to the subway station, swipe my Metro-Card, and by the time I'm on the train I've pulled myself together again. Well, except for the fact that my life is ruined. But other than that small detail, I'm fine.

What are the chances someone else will suddenly volunteer to be goalie? Like, ten percent, maybe?

Sigh.

8

I get home and am still so keyed up that I can't sit to do my homework or watch TV or anything. Dad is making a scary meat marinade in the kitchen and Mom is staying late at work, so I decide to be a caring big sister and see what Travis is up to in her room.

I find her hunkered over the family laptop; before I have a chance to see if she's making a Justin Bieber fan page or what, she sticks her tongue out at me and kicks the door shut in my face.

Well, that's lovely.

You know, sometimes it's like Travis and I live on different planets or something. Until I was about eleven, we used to have a blast together having sleepovers in each other's rooms, making cookie dough and eating it instead of baking it, hiding our parents' pillows in random places around the house. Dumb stuff, but still really fun at the time. Now we barely talk anymore unless she's barging into my room or whining about something. I don't know what she has to complain about, since pretty much everything goes her way all the time. Her only challenge in life is learning her multiplication tables, for crying out loud. And she slams the door in *my* face? Incredible.

I reach for my phone to call Cass, who I know will cheer me up by going off on how wretched Julie is . . . but it's not in my pocket. I search my backpack and come up with nothing. What the eff? Then I suddenly realize I left it on the table at the pizzeria. *Crap.* Luckily it's locked—like I'd really leave even a *chance* for someone to read my texts—but this means I have to turn around and go all the way back to Antonio's.

I contemplate leaving it till the morning and running in before classes start, but if someone takes it, my parents will kill me and say I'm not responsible and that I can't have another one. Then if I say, *What about safety?* they might give me one of those lame walkie-talkie things that Travis has, and then I will have to heave myself into a sewer to avoid being permanently ostracized at school. So I have no choice but to go now.

I yell to Dad that I'll be back in half an hour and walk three blocks back to the Seventh Avenue station to wait for the Manhattan-bound F train. I sit on a wooden bench and open my English book—*The Scarlet Letter*—to the dog-eared page and get about a paragraph in when I hear my name being called. I look up and see a guy across the platform waving at me.

Oh. My. God.

It's Jordan Rothman. He's making a gesture to me like "up and over," and I realize he's going to go up the stairs on his side, cross over, and come down to meet me on my side.

I quickly run my tongue over my teeth to make sure there's no oregano stuck in them—oh, God, why didn't I check the mirror before I left home?—and before I'm even sure, he's there, plunking down onto the bench next to me.

He's still in his soccer uniform and he looks so hot I can't even deal. What is it about guys who play soccer? They have the best bodies, period. Jordan smells like some kind of spicy men's deodorant, and his hair is a little sweaty and flopping over his forehead. He's grinning in that sort of sly way he has and his laser-beam eyes are focused directly on *me*.

I am dying. Totally and completely dying on the spot.

I somehow manage to smile (naturally, I hope) and say, "Hey, Jordan, what's up?" In my head I'm thinking, *Are you as happy as I am now that Jemma has been banished to parts unknown? Oh, and by the way, do you want to marry me?*

He says, "Nothing."

Hmm. Not much of an opening there. Why'd he come over here if he didn't have something to say?

"That's cool." *Oh, brilliant reply, Kelsey. Perfect.*

He points to my book. "Man, I can't believe you're actually reading that. Ever heard of CliffsNotes?"

"Yeah, it totally sucks," I say, even though to be honest I kind of like it. *Um . . . is this going somewhere?* Not that I wouldn't be happy to just sit here and stare at him until the train comes. Or forever. But still . . .

"So, anyway . . . me and my bro are having a Halloween party when the 'rents are out of town. You should come. Bring your friends or whatever."

I seriously can't believe this is happening. It's like the worst day of my life just became the *best* day of my life. Jordan Rothman just climbed a flight of stairs with the sole purpose of inviting *me* to a party? If the floor of the subway station weren't so disgusting, I think I'd totally faint.

Clearly this is some kind of sign. This year *is* going to be amazing—I knew it! Sure, the goalie thing is a bit of a hiccup, but I think getting my first real kiss from Jordan on Halloween will totally make up for it. Ah, sweet romance!

The train blasts into the station, so I shout to Jordan that I'll definitely plan to be there and manage to board the train without doing anything ridiculous like falling over with joy. I'm so psyched that I can't even read my book during the ride but just sit there staring at an MTA safety poster and imagining what it will be like to be alone with Jordan in the dark.

After envisioning about ten fantastic scenarios, I get off the train and practically float all the way to marvelous Antonio's, where I retrieve my phone from the darling, thoughtful cashier and turn around to go home again. Life is so delightful, I can't even believe it.

It isn't until I'm on the train again that I suddenly think, *Hey, I wonder what Jordan was doing in Brooklyn? He lives on the Upper East Side.*

Weird.

9

Julie Nelson is Satan incarnate. If I thought I hated her *before* I was goalie, it's nothing compared to now.

You know that dream where you have to complete a task—say, piling up rocks or something—but no matter how hard you try, you can't finish it? That's what soccer practice is like for me now. I stand for three hours a day, defenseless inside a giant net, while twenty girls kick hard rubber balls at me. And when I'm not doing that, I have to practice falling so I can (presumably) catch ground balls. Want to know what happens if you repeatedly fling yourself onto the ground? Your body is transformed into one giant bruise. I think I'm single-handedly supporting the Advil company at this point.

It's horrible.

As if my broken body and spirit aren't punishment enough, I still have to run at the start of practice, which makes approximately zero sense, since all I do is stand there watching my teammates dash around the rest of the time.

It was during our first game, which happened a mere ten days after I was given the news that my soccer career had been basically terminated, that I got to reevaluate a very important rule of the game: If, as goalie, you actually manage to catch the ball—which I miraculously did, exactly one time—the players on the opposing team are allowed to try and *take it from you* by kicking it out of your grasp. This is a rule I liked a lot better when I was on the other side of the net. All I could do was curl myself around the ball and hang on for dear life in a heap on the ground as a million cleats began swishing toward my head.

Oh, and by the way, you know what makes it extra easy to hang on to a slippery round ball? *Padded gloves.* Nothing like giant sock-hands to really give you an edge on the field.

After the game (we lost, of course), Coach Cantwell came up to me, thumped me on one of my mangled arms, and hollered, "Great reaction during that goal catch, Kelsey! Keep it up!" Keep what up, exactly? Following my fight-or-flight instinct?

I am so not cut out for this. I wonder if I could sign up for Ecology Club instead? I like nature. . . .

On Thursday afternoon (also known as Day Thirteen of Goalie Hell), I'm in my last-period English class. Keith Mayhew, my not-so-secret admirer, has spent the entire period distracting me from learning about Puritan adulteresses by covertly sending me funny text messages that I read under my desk.

I've just finished scrolling through a quite well written and incredibly rude limerick Keith texted about our teacher when the bell finally rings. I shove everything in my bag and make a break for the door, but there's no escape—Keith is right there as he always is after this class, trotting alongside me to my locker.

"So, Kels, y'know, you psyched for the game today? I bet you guys win this one," he says, with about a hundred times more enthusiasm than I feel. "Just don't think about the pain, y'know? Just throw yourself out there. That's what I do! Y'know?"

Incidentally, Keith runs track. And unless there's a new hurling-objects-at-sprinters category that I'm unaware of, I'm pretty sure I do *NOT* know.

"Yeah, thanks, Keith. Look, I have to get into my gear and stuff, so . . . see you tomorrow, okay?"

"Oh, I'm coming to watch you guys play—me and some of the guys, y'know? Show our school spirit, first home game and whatnot."

Oh, no. The last thing I want is for anyone to watch—

"Don't look all worried. I didn't make a big 'Kelsey' poster or anything."

Wow. That was something he considered?

"Oh, I didn't think . . . um, yeah. So, great, then. I mean,

I think it's not going to be that fun, though. So feel free to leave after about three minutes if you get bored." I slam my locker closed and grab my stuff. "Seriously, Keith. You don't—"

"C'mon, Kels, you're just nervous, y'know? You'll do great."

If I hear the words *you* or *know* one more time, I may have to burn the school to the ground. No, that's unfair—it's not Keith's fault. I'm just stressed-out and miserable.

I get to the locker room and change into my goalie gear—as far away from modelesque Lexi as possible, of course—and chat with the other girls a bit. We stretch and then huddle up for Julie's pregame pep talk, which ends with a charming "And Kelsey, try to catch something today, okay? Thanks much."

Sigh.

As I head for my net of despair, I hear my name being yelled. I look out to the bleachers and see Keith and some of his friends sitting with Em and JoJo. I wave at them, wondering where Cass is. Maybe she had an acting lesson? Or went to check out the guys' game on the other side of the field?

The whistle blasts, starting the game, and all my teammates spring into motion. As Lexi smoothly commandeers the ball, I stand there watching as the action quickly zips to the other end of the field. Well, good. The opposing team is rumored to be pretty terrible, so maybe my teammates will spend the whole time harassing *their* goalie and I can take a nice nap. Or perhaps make a festive dandelion chain.

About forty-five minutes later, we're making mincemeat out of them; the score is 6–0, and I haven't had the ball anywhere near me yet. Since I've essentially been a spectator this whole time, I'm actually enjoying myself—cheering my head off for my team and anticipating the delicious celebratory cupcakes we're sure to be eating after the game.

Suddenly, some horrible middy on the other team has the nerve to take control of the ball and actually gets past our defense. She's running right toward me and no one is on her.

Hello? This is no time to get lax, people! Don't you know there is no way I can stop her from scoring if she gets over here? Have we learned nothing from practice?!

I try to look intimidating as sweat rolls into my eyes. Great—now one of my contact lenses is all blurry. I ignore it and start sashaying awkwardly from side to side inside the goal. God, I suck at being goalie.

I can practically feel the girl breathing on me. My teammates are scrambling to catch up . . . they're close . . . but not close enough.

The girl kicks.

She catches the ball with her toe instead of the flat of her foot—and it's arcing like a basketball instead of going straight. I run underneath it, reach out, pray . . .

And catch it!

I caught something! And it was a ball! In your face, Julie Nelson!

My team freaks out, as do my friends in the stands. I turn my back for a sec so they don't all see me grinning my face off—after all, I still don't have any interest in being goalie—and suddenly, I'm flat on the ground.

I think my spine may be broken in several places. I can't breathe, so I drop the ball, which rolls into the goal. I hear a whistle and the ref yelling, "Time-out!"

Then our center forward, a sophomore named Steli, is hauling me up to my feet. I can hear one of the other girls screaming somewhere behind me, "Are you crazy? She cleated her right in the back! That's a totally illegal goal! What the hell, Ref?!"

"Did that girl *kick* me?" I wheeze.

Ana comes over and hands me some water. "Yeah, that bitch," Steli is saying. "And she didn't even get a yellow card! That team must be connected to the ref or something. You okay?"

"Yeah, I think I just got the wind knocked out of me." I glance over to the stands and see Em and JoJo looking in my direction nervously, miming that they want to come make sure I'm okay. I wave at them to let them know I am. Keith is making a gesture I can only assume means "Don't think about the pain, y'know?" but could just as easily mean "I'm a harmonica chicken!"

As my lungs start working again, I notice the scoreboard

now reads 6–1. *What?!* "They gave them the goal? That's so unfair!"

"I know," Ana agrees, fuming. "Cantwell is arguing. We'll still win the game, though, don't worry. There's only a few minutes left."

I'm reconciling the fact that, since there's no sub for me, I'm going to have to get back in the stupid net and finish the game, when Captain Julie comes storming in my direction. She looks furious, and I'm guessing it's not because she's upset that I got injured.

"Kelsey! Do you realize we could've had our first shutout if you hadn't dropped the ball *again*? The team is counting on you to guard the goal and you *suck* at it!"

Very nice. Do I have to respond to this?

"Julie, Kelsey just got kicked in the back! No one could've held on to that ball," Steli says, rushing to my defense.

"Was I talking to you? Get back to your position." Julie glares at me. "You know, I took a chance giving you Katie's spot as goalie and you're totally screwing it up. I have no idea why Cantwell put you on JV. Seriously."

I open my mouth, ready to throw caution to the wind (she already hates me, so what harm can it do?) and say something along the lines of *I didn't want this stupid job, you jerk!* but before I can go through with it, the whistle blows and Julie stomps off back to her position.

And so ends another terrific day in the life of Kelsey Finkelstein, Goalie Extraordinaire. Hooray.

10

"But, Kels, there are *five* Village People," Cassidy insists, reaching past me for another bottle of Smirnoff Ice. "We can't just have four. That would be like . . . weird."

I take a swig out of my bottle and grimace. It's sickly sweet, but it gets the job done. Anyway, it's what Cass's older brother Nathan had leftover from some party last week, and it was free, so we'll take it.

We're in Cass's room on Saturday night; we were supposed to go out and do something awesome, except we couldn't think of anything. None of us besides JoJo has a fake ID, and even if we did, we don't have enough money to go anywhere cool. Contrary to what TV producers seem to think, fourteen-year-olds aren't exactly sought after in the world of NYC nightlife.

Besides—I just want to forget all about the horrible game two days ago and think about Halloween, Jordan's party, and hooking up. Not necessarily in that order.

"Cass," I counter, "unless you want to be the weird motorcycle guy or can find someone who does, we're having four. Come on—no one will know the difference! And female Village People is such a killer idea. You know you want to wear a sexy feather headdress."

Actually, *I* want to wear a sexy feather headdress. But sometimes you have to make sacrifices to get a concept together.

JoJo snickers. She's lying facedown on Cass's bed, sifting through a makeup bag full of Manic Panic bottles. She picks out an orange one and rolls it between her palms. "I'm being the Cowgirl," she declares. "I found these crazy leather chaps of my mom's in a random trunk last week, and they're hilarious. What about you, Em?"

"I'm okay with whatever," Em murmurs, her thumbs moving a mile a minute on the keyboard of her phone. She's been texting James constantly all night.

"Or you could dress up as a YMCA. Like, the actual building. We could make your costume out of a big cardboard box!" JoJo suggests, knowing Em hasn't heard a word we've said all night. Cass and I giggle.

"Sure, that's great," Em agrees, still texting.

"Hello? Earth to Em?" I ask, reaching over to tap the screen of her phone.

Em finally looks up, blushing. "Sorry, sorry. I know—I'm becoming 'that girl' . . . I'll stop. It's just that I really—"

"Miss James!" we chant in unison.

Em flushes an even brighter red than before. Poor Em— she's so easy to tease. She snaps the phone shut decisively and puts it in her bag. "Okay, I'm done. Seriously. Now, what were we talking about?"

"Um, the night that is going to transform this year from horror to awesomeness? The turning point in my life, which has thus far been, well, *less* than awesome?"

"Oh, right, Halloween. How could I forget?" Em giggles and reaches for her can of soda. She never drinks alcohol, which is one thing we *don't* tease her about. She's always afraid people will think she's a loser for not liking to drink, which of course is silly but happens all the time anyway.

"Cass thinks we need five Village People," JoJo explains, "even though we think four is enough. What do you think?"

"I can't even *name* all five Village People and we've been discussing this for days, so I think it will be fine. Can I be the cop?"

"Mmmm," Cass mumbles. We glance over and see that Cass is now reading a text of her own. "What? Oh, yeah. I want to be the Indian."

"Who are you texting over there, woman? Everyone good is already here!" JoJo tries to snatch the phone away, but Cass is too fast for her. She shoves it into the pocket of her jeans.

"Who are you texting—a guy? How could you not tell us about this?" I demand. Unbelievable! Cass is withholding hookup information? Cass is the world's biggest gossip—she doesn't believe in secrets. That's one of my very favorite things about her!

"I . . . uh . . . don't want to jinx anything, okay? Just let it go." Cass takes a swig of her Smirnoff Ice. "Ugh—this stuff is terrible. Nathan's friends have the worst taste in the world."

"I kind of like it, actually." JoJo shrugs, taking a sip of her own. "And don't change the subject."

I step in. "If she doesn't want to talk about it, we don't have to talk about it." JoJo can be relentless, and Cass is obviously uncomfortable for some reason. Does she have a weird crush on someone gross, like Danny Zifner? Oh my God, I want to know so badly! But then Cass shoots me a grateful look, so I try to contain my curiosity. "Let's talk about me making out with Jordan instead."

Everyone groans.

"Fiiine!" I exclaim. "Just forget it. I give up! You guys plan Halloween. I'll be over here, crying quietly in the corner . . ."

And that's how, despite coming up with the awesome idea in the first place—with every intention of rocking a sexy Indian Princess costume—I ended up getting stuck with Construction Worker. Which is almost as bad as Weird Motorcycle Guy.

At least I have permission to go to Jordan's party. Well, really I have permission to sleep over at JoJo's, which is what I always do when there's a party or something my parents would never let me go to. JoJo's parents might as well still be in high school themselves; they're always making out and smoking pot and stuff. The important thing is, I will be at Jordan's house next Saturday night. And it will be life changing. I can feel it.

On Wednesday after dinner, I realize I'm completely out of blackhead-removing pore strips, which are essential if I'm going to look perfect for the party. I head out to the Duane Reade Pharmacy near my house around nine P.M., and when I get up to the counter to pay, there's Jordan. Oh my God. This is a sign, right? I mean, the party is in three days, it's pretty much all I can think about, and here he is. I manage to not actually skip with glee as I approach him.

"Heeeeeey, Kelsey." He takes his bag of purchases from the counter. "What's up?"

Even his *voice* is hot. I try not to giggle. "Oh, you know. The usual. Homework. Pore strips." *Ack! Did I just say "pore strips" to Jordan Rothman?* I attempt to distract him, asking, "So, um, what are you doing in Brooklyn?"

"Oh, uh, I had to get this thing but they didn't have it in my neighborhood, and, uh, I had to come get it at this one because, uh, they had it. Or whatever."

Well, that's sort of odd. There are about a thousand Duane Reades in the city. I consider pointing this out, but why question fate? Obviously the universe is conspiring to bring us together, and if the Park Slope Duane Reade is the venue, I'm certainly not going to argue. Besides, I'm too busy screaming inside my head, *OH MY GOD, I LOVE YOU!*

I pay for my stuff and walk with him to the train stop. I can practically feel the electricity between us. Surely he can feel it too, because he asks, "So, are you guys coming to my party or what?"

"Sure, I guess," I reply, as though I just remembered he even invited me, to which he responds, "Cool." *Ah, very smooth. Excellent, Kelsey—good work!*

"So, um, I guess I'll see you tomorrow. And at the party, obviously. Guess what? We're going as the Village—"

"Yeah, hey, the train's coming, so I gotta run. 'Kay, see you later!" he calls, running down the stairs. Well, it's not like he was going to miss the train just to chat some more. I'm not his girlfriend or anything—*yet!*

I mean, obviously he really wants me to come to the party. So he'll probably ask me out by the end of the night. Or at least kiss me. Right?

As I walk home, I start thinking: Why *was* he in Brooklyn on a school night? Besides the Hand of Fate, there has to be a real, logical reason, and I'm coming up blank. The only explanation I can ultimately think of is that Jordan has been secretly in love with me all along, trapped by cruel Jemma Bradley in a web of lies and deception, waiting for the chance to break free of her insidious clutches. And now he's following me around Park Slope, lurking in local stores and train stations, desperately trying to get up the courage to come clean. And why couldn't that be the case? It makes perfect sense to *me*.

The second I get home, I call each of my friends in turn to lay out my brilliant theory. I spend all night discussing Jordan's creativity, devotion, and willingness to travel to a different borough for love. Interestingly enough, JoJo doesn't think Jordan could actually plan something that elaborate, and Cass keeps trying to change the subject to her Indian headdress (which, apparently, is proving harder to find than she'd anticipated). Em, of course, is totally on board with my theory. And anyway, the more I think about it, the more obvious it seems that our moment—mine and Jordan's, that is—is finally here.

The party will be the big test.

11

Saturday night, we arrive at Jordan's apartment fashionably late, and immediately I can see we're in the minority, agewise—it's mostly his brother's friends, who are juniors and seniors. I realize that means Cap'n Julie is probably here, and suddenly I feel grateful that my giant yellow Construction Worker hat covers half my face. Before we got here, I'd been thinking how ridiculous it looked, but now? I almost wish it were even bigger.

Some guy hands me a stack of red plastic cups and I pass them out to my friends—oh, did I mention how totally awesome we look? Cassidy's headdress is dripping feathers everywhere, and Em's dad got her an actual policeman's hat and badge from their local precinct. Plus JoJo found an old fringed leather vest to go with the bizarre chaps. We are very fabulous and authentic, especially compared to the other costumes on display at this party, which are extremely lame. I mean, a cat? A fairy? Does anyone have an imagination anymore?

We go to the kitchen and discover there are a bunch

of kegs in there. I had my first beer at a slumber party in seventh grade, and in my opinion it tastes like dog urine, but since it's pretty much the only beverage choice, I figure I'll just carry it around and pretend to drink it so as not to look like a total loser. Which is really sad, since why should I have to drink beer to look cool? More importantly, have these people never heard of wine coolers? Even Smirnoff Ice would be better than beer. Oh, well.

I fill my cup with beer and take a tiny sip. *Eeeyuch*. It's actually kind of weird to me that we're going to parties with kegs now. I mean, sure, we sneak alcohol when we hang out at each other's houses and stuff, and a few people spiked their drinks at some of the eighth-grade graduation parties last year. But this is new territory, being at a party with older kids and no parents and everyone drinking right out in the open. It's sort of exciting and dangerous feeling at the same time.

Of course, if my parents had any idea, I would be deader than a doornail.

After a while I decide to take a lap around the party to see who's there, i.e., to find and corner Jordan. Even though I'm wearing a huge plastic hat, I figure can still make the most of my feminine wiles. I applied lots of charcoal eyeliner and lash-extending mascara when I was getting ready, so I start batting my eyes a lot to call attention to them.

Within about thirty seconds, I get a makeup-coated eyelash on my contact lens, which is just about the most painful thing in the entire world. It's like having a knife plunged into your eye. So I'm sort of clutching my face, trying to shove through witches and vampires to find the bathroom, when I walk right into Lexi.

Of course she's dressed as a sexy schoolgirl. And she looks more gorgeous than ever in her teensy kilt and white button-down shirt tied in a knot above her perfect abs. I can practically feel every guy there having a heart attack, especially with the perfectly contrasting backdrop of me in a yellow hard hat, rubbing at my eye like a maniac.

I wait for Lexi to say something like, *Hi! Aren't I the most fabulous person in the whole world? Don't look now, but I'm going to poke you in the one eye you've got left and run away laughing!* But instead she gasps, "Oh my God, is it your contact? I *hate* when that happens!"

She guides me to the bathroom, where she rummages around till she finds some saline solution. Then she sits on the toilet and says, "Ugh, I've had glasses since second grade and I had these gross red frames my mom made me get. They were beyond hideous and everyone made fun of me, so I was soooo psyched to get contacts in middle school. They can be such a pain, though. You should try waterproof mascara next time, maybe."

Of course, I'm thinking, *Lexi wears glasses?* and *People teased Lexi? For real? How awesome!* But then I feel bad, so I just say, "Yeah, that's a good idea. Thanks."

Lexi asks, "Do you ever freak out your friends by moving your contact in your eye?"

"Yes! All the time—Em thinks it's the nastiest thing ever."

Lexi laughs and starts touching her contact lens in her eye and making this awful puking face and now I'm laughing, too.

Then we realize we're in Jordan's and Seth's bathroom, so we go through the medicine cabinet and find really weird stuff in it like nose-hair clippers and milk of magnesia and a crusty bottle of little-kid cough syrup that looks about a hundred years old.

"Maybe I should give these tweezers to Julie," I suggest, holding up a pair. "She could certainly use them."

"Oh, yeah, definitely. I think that will really help your relationship." Lexi giggles, takes a compact out of her tiny purse, and starts reapplying her lip gloss.

I sigh. "I'm never going to get out of being goalie, am I?"

"Well . . . maybe someone will volunteer?"

"Yeah, right." I finish wiping off the smeared mascara from under my eyes with a tissue and turn to Lexi. "Ready to go?"

Lexi holds up her hand to stop me from opening the door. "Actually, Kelsey, can I tell you something?"

"Um . . . sure. What's up?" *This is weird. What could she possibly have to—*

"This might sound super lame, but I think you're really

cool and funny . . . and even though I've sort of inherited my cousin's friends, it's still hard to be the new girl, you know? Anyway, I thought maybe . . . we could hang out sometime after practice or something?"

I'm so shocked that my mouth actually falls open for a second, just like in a cartoon. I quickly close it. Wow. It certainly never occurred to me that I'd ever end up bonding with Lexi in a bathroom next to my crush's foot fungus cream, but here we are. Maybe Em was right about her— she *is* really nice. And thinks I'm awesome, apparently. Was I too quick to judge her because of horrible Jemma?

I sputter, "No, I mean, yes—of course we should. That would be great." And as a matter of fact, it would be. It really is amazing how a chuckle over cough syrup and a few compliments can make you forget the intense dislike you've held for someone for over a month, isn't it?

Unless I find out she is having sex with Jordan. Or even just making out with him.

Then I will have to destroy her.

Lexi and I grab our red cups, I slap my hard hat back on, and we leave the bathroom, only to discover there's a line of people down the hall waiting. From around the corner, out of sight, I hear a huffy "Finally! What, did you forget which way a tampon goes or something?" and recognize the obnoxious voice of Julie Nelson. I start to tug Lexi in the other direction when Cass comes dashing past.

Her headdress is kind of a mess and her Indian makeup is smeared.

What has she been up to? Something with a mysterious text buddy, perhaps?

Before I have time to check out the near vicinity for clues, Cass sees me and practically squeals, "Kels, there you are! Let's go get another drink!"

Julie, her eyebrows (which really enhance what I assume is a very convincing Frida Kahlo outfit), and Ned Garman come stomping over, presumably to see what the holdup by the bathroom is. Ned isn't even wearing a costume—he has on the same black outfit he always wears.

Julie glares at us, turns to Ned, and sneers, "Oh my God. They let *freshmen* into this party? How pathetic! Does Seth know about this?" She gulps down some of her drink. "No offense, Lexi."

"Um, Jordan invited us personally, for your infor—," Cass starts unsteadily.

"Cass, come on, let's just go back to the party," I hiss. I grab her arm—the last thing I need is to deal with Julie right now. A full-on scene will not help Mission Makeout at all.

Cass scowls at Julie and theatrically links her arm through mine. Unfortunately, she knocks against the hand holding my still-full cup of beer, which splashes all over the front of Julie's shirt.

She starts shrieking, "My shirt! This is Zac Posen, you stupid idiot!" To *me*, by the way, not Cassidy, who of course slinks away from the scene.

"Oh my God, Julie, I'm so sorry." I gulp. "It was an accident. I'll pay for the dry cleaning, I'll give you my soul, whatever!" But she just screams wordlessly in my face and storms off with Ned in tow.

At this point Em comes up and says, "There you are—oh, hi, Lexi! Listen, Kels, did you leave your purse downstairs? I think some guy may have just puked on it. And did you find you-know-who yet? Because Keith Mayhew is asking everyone where you are and half the people here think he's your boyfriend. Just so you know . . ."

And a very happy Halloween to me.

12

So that was pretty much the Halloween party. We decided to cut our losses shortly thereafter and grab a cab back to JoJo's—all before I even *saw* Jordan, much less made out with him. So much for believing in miracles. I seriously don't understand where he could have been all night that I didn't see him even *once*. And after all my careful planning . . .

I am trying, despite everything, to retain my cheerful demeanor. Another opportunity to hook up with Jordan is around the corner—it has to be. Positive thinking is hard, but I'm really working on it.

You know what would help? A big bag of free candy. Maybe I should've just gone trick-or-treating with Travis and called it a night.

Anyway, now it's back to the daily grind, looking forward to Thanksgiving, winter break, and of course, the end of the tragic soccer season.

Soccer sucks.

Most years, my heart breaks at the thought of the season

coming to an end. This year, I'm literally counting the days till the last horrible game is over. Ever since the cleating incident, I'm not only bored inside the net but terrified as well, which means my performance as goalie has *not* improved. The only games we've won all season have been the ones where the other team is so awful they don't get anywhere near our goal, which is to say, me. I thought for sure Coach Cantwell would make somebody else take over after I helped us lose a stunning six games in a row, but she seems determined to "build up my confidence" and "not give up on me."

Oh, how I wish she would.

The only reason everyone on the team hasn't murdered me is because they know it's not strictly my fault. Even so, everyone on defense has to work twice as hard because I'm so tragically useless, and it's pretty tense in the locker room.

Since the Halloween party, Julie won't even speak to me—not even to yell. She just glares, her eyebrows waggling ferociously. I'm honestly not sure what's worse, frankly.

Next year, I may have to take up tennis.

After a couple weeks of not much else going on (November really is the most boring month, except for maybe March), I'm heading to meet Em by her locker before lunch when I'm intercepted by Keith. I can see from down the hall that

Em is texting away and not in a hurry to go, so I stop and say, "Hey, Keith. What's up?"

"Oh . . . y'know. Glad to be back in school. That E. coli thing really blew."

"Right, I heard about that. I'm glad you're feeling better." I glance at Em. Still devotedly texting. Doesn't James have school? I try to catch her eye for a swift rescue, but no luck. "So, uh . . . got any big plans for the weekend?"

"Yeah, well, y'know, the Foreign Scarves are playing on Saturday night, so, y'know . . . I'm gonna check that out."

I *love* the Foreign Scarves—they are, without question, my number one favorite band right now. People have been buzzing about the concert this weekend for ages. Unfortunately, the cheapest tickets are like eighty bucks, so I will *not* be attending.

"Keith, that is so fantastic!" I gush. "Oh my God, I'm so jealous of you right now. How'd you get tickets?" Keith looks a bit shocked—I guess this is the most excitement I've ever expressed in his direction.

"Well, my dad works for Sony, y'know, so he gets tickets to stuff all the time. They're a pretty cool group—"

"They are the *best*. Have you heard their new live album? I am obsessed with the fourth track—JoJo burned it for me and I listen to it constantly. You are so lucky!" This is just *typical*—of course Keith's dad works at Sony while mine works for Boring & Lame, Partners at Law. All I ever get from there are free legal pads to do homework on. Yippee.

"Anyway, so I have this extra ticket and I figured, y'know, you probably had plans, but if you wanted to go, maybe . . . ?"

And just like that, the clouds part and the sun is shining on me once again. My life is not going to be a total disaster from start to finish!

I basically have a total meltdown all over Keith, which I'm now very worried has given him the wrong idea. But I'm just so excited that I can't help it! The Foreign Scarves—live! I seriously cannot wait.

I thank Keith about sixteen times and tell him I'll e-mail him later to figure out the details. Then I zip over to Em's locker and pry her away from her phone to tell her the great news as we walk to the cafeteria.

". . . and the best part is, maybe Jordan will hear that I'm going to the concert with Keith and Jordan'll think it's a date and then it'll, like, spur him on a bit to ask me out himself. Don't you think?"

"Sure, Kels, but . . . does *Keith* think this is a date? Because you don't want to hurt his feelings, right?"

"No, of course I don't! I've made it clear a million times that we're just friends. And of course I wouldn't want to make him feel bad—you know I like Keith. It's just that he's, well . . . Keith."

We go inside and grab chairs at our usual table. JoJo is already there, chatting to some friends and chowing down. Her bangs are bright pink today, and she's wearing an asymmetrical shirt that has one long sleeve and one spaghetti strap. I'd look like a total poser in it, but JoJo looks great.

"Hey, cool shirt!" Em says, pulling a sandwich out of her brown paper bag.

"Oh, thanks—I made it last night. Just playing around with my mom's old sewing machine."

"I love that you were 'playing around' and made an actual shirt that looks good. Anyone else would've made a muumuu or something, probably," I point out.

"What can I say?" JoJo grins. She opens her mouth to add something else, but I can't hold it in—I'm ready to burst with my news.

"I'm going to see the Foreign Scarves on Saturday!" I scream as quietly as possible. (We are, after all, still freshmen, i.e., the lowest rung on the cafeteria totem pole.) Predictably, everyone at the table goes wild.

"How did you get tickets?" JoJo demands. "The show is totally sold out—even my dad couldn't get me any!"

Oh, how I wish I could say something like *Oh, you know, Jordan and I are going in a stretch Hummer. After the show we're going to swing by SoHo House for a quiet drink. After that, well . . . I really shouldn't say . . .* Instead I mumble into my applesauce, "Keith is taking me."

"Keith is taking you where?" Cass asks as she slides into the seat next to me. She's a bit out of breath and her hair is messy, like she ran all the way to the caf or something. Odd.

"The Foreign Scarves concert!"

"Oh my God, I'm going too!" she squeals.

"You *are*?!" JoJo sputters. "How'd *you* get a ticket?"

"And why didn't you tell us?!" Em demands.

"Oh, uh . . . Nathan gave me a ticket. For my birthday. An early birthday present," Cass says, looking kind of uncomfortable. "He just gave it to me, like, yesterday, but then I had that Spanish test, so I forgot to—"

"Uh, Nathan, your *brother*?" I cut in. "As in, the guy who usually gives you something he already owns and doesn't want anymore? *That* Nathan?"

"Yeah, well . . . he felt bad about that. I mean, he's my brother. Don't badmouth him, Kelsey, okay?" Cass takes a bite of her pear and turns away from me. Well, now I feel bad—but she's the one who brings that stuff up all the time. She can't stand her brother!

"Cass, I was only kidding. You know I didn't—"

"Whatever, it's fine," she says, chewing. We fall into an awkward silence.

"Well, I have something to share," JoJo finally says, breaking the tension. "Something I think you will be very interested in, Kels." She reaches into her bag, pulls out a newspaper, and hands it to me.

I look down and see it's the new issue of *The Reflector*. I look at JoJo questioningly.

"Hot off the presses! Doesn't officially come out till tomorrow, but I've got an inside connection."

"Your parents must be so proud." Em laughs.

"Anywaaaay," JoJo continues, pointing at me, "I thought you'd want to know that you made the big time again. Our little star . . . But this time you're off the hook, so don't worry."

"JoJo, what the heck are you talking about?" I ask.

"Turn to the sports section."

I turn to the last page of the paper and gasp. There, splashed across the page, is a headline that reads: GIRLS' JV SOCCER GAME ENDS WITH BOGUS CALL. Under that is an article, and next to the article is a huge picture—a truly spectacular action shot.

Of me.

In my goalie outfit, right at the moment of impact when that awful middy cleated me in the back *weeks* ago. Why? Why is the *Reflector* staff out to get me? Stupid school paper. Stupid retroactive reporting! Couldn't they find anything else to write about? Cass glances over at the picture and giggles.

I no longer feel bad about dissing her brother.

"Well, if you'll all excuse me, I'm going to go torch the *Reflector* office," I manage to say through gritted teeth. "Then I'm going to write a warm thank-you note to"—I squint at the teensily printed photo credit under the picture; yup, it's the same generic STAFF PHOTOGRAPHER as the first one—"whoever, thank him or her for giving me my second beautiful moment in the paper, and respectfully request that it be my last. Why don't they have photo credits? This is the worst newspaper I've ever seen!" I crumple the page up, mentally formulating a plan to go flush my head down a toilet in the girls' bathroom.

"Kelsey, wait! You missed the most important part!" JoJo grabs the paper back, smoothes it out, and points to the caption. It reads: JV Goalie Katie Stolting Viciously Attacked By Opposing Player.

I scan the article, and the whole thing is about Katie. Ha! Whoever wrote it must have looked at the old team roster from before Katie broke her ankle—so no one will know that it's me! I sink back into my seat with relief. I may have led the team in a downward spiral as far as the season goes, but at least it's not on the record.

"This is great!" Em exclaims. "I mean, not really *great*, but . . . you know. It's kind of weird, actually. Shouldn't the newspaper be up on fact-checking and everything? I mean, I know it's only a school paper and the news is always out-of-date and stuff, but still . . ."

"Well, I think in this case it's definitely for the best," I say.

Of course, that really is a tragic photo of me. Maybe I can go see if it's too late to change it? Perhaps to a nice shot of Julie looking mean and scary?

"Hey, guys—got room for one more?"

It's Lexi, hovering next to our table with her tray. She often sits with us, but she always asks first if it's okay—like we might say no. Does she not realize that she could sit anywhere she wanted without asking, even with the seniors if she felt like it? Perfect people really are a mystery.

"Of course!" I smile. I slide over so she can squeeze in between me and Em. "Here's what you missed—Cass and I are going to the Scarves concert on Saturday, and JoJo has an inside connection at the school paper. Major stuff."

"Seriously?" Lexi asks. "That's awesome—I saw them in LA last summer and they *killed*." Then she turns to JoJo. "I've actually been thinking about submitting an article or something to the newspaper—I used to write for the one at my old school. What's your big connection, JoJo?"

JoJo laughs. "Nothing, actually! Someone just left a copy of the new edition in the computer lab."

"I'm pretty sure *The Reflector* would welcome you—or anyone even remotely literate, for that matter—with open arms," I tell Lexi. "Why don't you just go to the next meeting or e-mail the editor or something?"

"Yeah, maybe . . . I just feel weird about walking in and being like, 'Hi, can I please be part of your club?' or whatever."

"Lexi. Are you serious? There are at least seven guys staring at you right now, as we speak. You've been here less than three months and everyone worships you. Why would you feel weird to go into the newspaper office?"

Lexi fiddles with her sandwich crusts and shrugs. "I'm not good at putting myself out there, you know? I dunno . . . I guess I'm just shy about that stuff." She brightens, putting her hand on my arm. "Hey—would you go with me? Then I wouldn't feel like such a dork."

I've said it before and I'll say it again: I just don't understand this girl. I like her, now that I've gotten to know her. But I do not get her at all. How could she ever feel like a dork? She knows she could win *America's Next Top Model* without even auditioning for the show, right? Could this possibly be a brilliant fake-out? Is she in cahoots with Julie Nelson?

But she seems serious.

"Uh, yeah, if you want me to, sure. Why not?"

My phone buzzes in my pocket and I open it up to a text from Em, less than three feet away. It reads: See? I told you she was nice!

13

So, tonight is the Foreign Scarves concert, and there are some major questions to be answered. Such as: What should I wear? How can I make sure Keith doesn't mistake this totally platonic outing for an evening of romance? What are the chances the band will spot me in the crowd and pull me on stage with them?

I call Em for a fashion consultation, and after a lot of back and forth, we agree on a perfect outfit. I wriggle into my new jeans and an amazing wrap sweater that I got with my Urban Outfitters gift card. I apply eyeliner in fabulous smoky-eye fashion, flatiron my hair, and dab on mint-infused, subtly tinted lip balm.

I'm ready.

Of course my lame dad insists that I have to take a car to the club with someone because the subway at night is too dangerous. Well, I certainly don't want to go with Keith—that would seem very date-like, I think. Better to meet him there. I convince Cass to come over to my house so we can go together—despite what she said at lunch the other day, I know she doesn't want to go with her gross brother.

My mother is heading to a late work meeting of some sort and is devastated to only have a few minutes to gush about my "First Adult Dating Experience," which, based on the eighty-seven photos my dad snaps with his new digital camera, is actually with Cass. My attempts to point out for the millionth time that this is not, in fact, a date fall on deaf ears.

We *finally* leave. The second we get in the car, Cass goes, "So, do you think you'll hook up with Keith tonight?"

"Cass, this is *not*—"

"I know, I know—it's not a date. But still, like . . . maybe you'll change your mind?"

"Um, no, I will *not* change my mind, unless Keith magically transforms into Jordan. Besides, even if there were no Jordan, Keith is too short. And there's that freaky eye thing . . ."

"Kels, there is no eye thing. Keith's eyes are totally normal."

"Cass, what's your deal? I'm not into Keith. He's nice, don't get me wrong, but I don't like him like that! Are you new?"

Cass flops back in her seat, pouting. "Okay, fine, just asking. Don't freak out or anything. Geeeeeez." She passes me the water bottle she brought, which is filled with cranberry juice and the three drops of vodka she managed to swipe. I think the driver is onto us, but he doesn't say anything.

At the door to the club, we get the humiliating stamps that mark us as underage, and I text Keith, who comes out to find me. He looks nice, I guess, but he's still no Jordan. Cass goes to find her brother, who is up in the nosebleed section somewhere, and Keith and I elbow our way to our unbelievable floor seats.

Keith talks a mile a minute throughout the sucky opening band and I learn that he used to make model airplanes (weird), is allergic to melon (weirder), and wants to go to Yale (are people already thinking about college?). Sheesh. I didn't know there was going to be quite so much sharing. So, what—am I supposed to show him the scar I got ice-skating and reveal my childhood fantasy of working at the McDonald's drive-thru window?

He hands me a little flask with his dad's initials on it, and I take some and pass it back. Then there's an earsplitting blast of feedback, all the lights go out, and a single spotlight hits the stage. The whole audience is silent, waiting, and when the Foreign Scarves finally come on, we all basically lose our minds. Everyone is bouncing around and dancing and mouthing the words to the first song, which is one of my all-time favorites.

I take a second to glance around and see if I can spot Cass, but I don't see her. Keith looks over at me and grins—oh,

Lord. Did he think I was looking at *him*? He starts dancing very close to me and sort of flinging his arms around in a bizarre way, then offers me some gum for about the sixth time.

I suddenly realize that there is no getting around it: Keith Mayhew is going to try to kiss me.

Craaaaaap. What do I do now? It's not like this is totally unfamiliar territory—I could've hooked up in middle school, with Keith or someone else I wasn't that interested in. I just . . . I wanted my first kiss to be special, so I never let it happen. I mean, I think it's a big deal, even if everyone says it doesn't matter. But how long am I supposed to wait for Jordan to get it together? And should I maybe get some practice in before he does? But if I *do* make out with Keith, will I be able to live with the knowledge that I abandoned my fantasy of the perfect first kiss just because I didn't want to be branded some kind of fourteen-year-old prude? And is this going to be a prolonged, tonguing sort of affair or just a kind of pecking situation?

And then, before I can finish reviewing the complete list of pros and cons, Keith goes for it. He lunges in, and suddenly his tongue is flopping around inside my mouth like a fish dying on a dock.

I think I may be choking to death. He tastes like . . . rum and Coke and spearmint gum. And panic. If a tongue could sweat, I think his would be.

I extricate myself from his clutches and manage to squeak, "Keith! What are you *doing*?"

"Sorry, sorry. I couldn't help it, Kelsey—you just look so hot tonight, y'know?"

Of course he has now said the perfect thing (note to self: wear smoky eyeliner every day from now on, even while sleeping) and I figure, *Okay—I might as well give it another shot*. So I kiss *him*, brimming with empowered-woman confidence.

And it is still *totally* awful!

What the hell? On TV it's all delicate and nice-looking with the rare big slurpy-yet-sexy moment, but *nothing* like this mess. My chin is all wet and I think I'm going to barf if he doesn't stop gagging me with his tongue. This can't be right; he must be doing it wrong.

I pull back, and he goes, "What's wrong?"

"Look, I don't think you're doing this right," I tell him. "It's way too much tongue or . . . something." I attempt to wipe some of the spit off my cheek with my shoulder in a way that I hope isn't too obvious. Blech.

Keith glares at me and shouts over the band, "Well, it's more like *you're* not doing it right. Have you ever even made out before? My brother is in *college*, y'know, and he told me everything there is to know about Frenching when we were in seventh grade, so I *think* I know what I'm doing, Kelsey. But don't worry—I'm happy to practice with you till you feel more confident about your skills."

First of all: Did he just say *Frenching*? Seriously? And second of all: He's happy to *practice* with me? Really? Well, how thoughtful! Maybe I'll buy him a model-airplane kit as a thank-you for his kind attention to my kissing education.

Yeah. I'll get right on that.

I look at him witheringly for a sec and then say, "Keith, I have to go to the bathroom. I'll be back." Of course, getting to the bathroom in this place will probably take an hour, which should give me enough time to think of a way to convincingly act like this never happened.

I wonder if you can decide to be a kissing virgin again. No one saw. What if I pretend I didn't just have a gross foreign tongue in my intestines and issue myself a well-deserved do-over?

I shove through a million people and finally make it to what is clearly the world's longest bathroom line. I take my phone out of my pocket, contemplating sending a text to Em. But what can I say in a text that could possibly convey the level of anxiety I'm currently dealing with? Writing *GAAAAAAAAH!!!* just about sums up my feelings but might be somewhat unclear. Better to call her later when I've figured out what my story is, anyway.

I look back toward the stage, where the lead guitarist is playing an unbelievable improvised solo. I cannot believe I'm missing it! Stupid Keith. Stupid *me*.

I scope out the line again, which is down to about half a million people now. I move forward two inches. My pocket buzzes with a text from Keith, which reads: R U coming back? I respond: Huge line, and snap the phone shut.

The two girls in front of me start giggling, pointing up at the balcony behind us, and I look up to see what's so funny: it's a couple making out like they just invented it. Is that how I looked when I was with Keith? Horrors.

The guy starts sucking his partner's neck like a crazed vampire, and one of the girls ahead of me in line snorts derisively.

"I know, get a room, right?" I say to her. It's always nice to make friends in the bathroom line.

"Seriously!" she replies. "I mean, if you're gonna spend a hundred bucks, it might as well involve a bed, right?"

I laugh, looking back up at the balcony. Then the stage lights do a sweep over the audience, and for a moment, the girl's face is illuminated.

It's Cassidy. *My* Cassidy.

And she's kissing . . .

Jordan Rothman.

My stomach drops to my knees.

14

I feel like I'm in a vacuum—there's absolutely no sound. And my eyes aren't working right; it's like, instead of being twenty feet above my head, Cassidy's and Jordan's faces are right in front of me, kissing passionately in slow motion so I can see every little detail.

I'm vaguely aware that the girl I was talking to is asking me something like, "Uh, are you okay?" but I can't pull my eyes away from the carnage of my romantic expectations. I may, in fact, be paralyzed. Except for my stomach, which feels like it's being kicked repeatedly.

I am *not* going to cry.

How, and in what world, is this even possible? Cassidy has *always* known how I feel about Jordan. She and I just talked about it on the way here!

I suddenly have a horrifying realization: My brilliant, hope-filled Jordan-Brooklyn theory is actually true. Only it doesn't involve me . . . it's been about *Cassidy* the whole time. She lives six blocks away from me with her dad, who is never home. Perfect after-school makeout opportunity. No wonder Cass was trying to steer me toward Keith!

Then all the little moments from the last couple of months start adding up. How could I have been so dumb? The texts Cass didn't want to talk about . . . disappearing at the Halloween party . . . that's why I didn't see Jordan—he was probably in his bedroom with Cass the whole time! Missing my soccer game when he was playing on the other field . . . even making me feel guilty at lunch the other day when she was obviously trying to cover up the fact that she had just been doing it with Jordan in the home ec lab or something.

And saying Nathan gave her a ticket to the concert tonight? Did I actually fall for that?

I furiously push my way back to Keith and I'm like, *Kiss me, you fool!* (I do not actually say this.) We proceed to make out like crazy, which is still totally wretched, but it's the most distracting thing I can think of. I am a pillar of strength in the face of adversity.

You know, you hear about groups of friends who split apart in high school for one reason or another, but I never thought it would happen to us. Sure, my relationship with Cass isn't quite as close as the one I have with Em, but I never thought in a million years that Cass would stab me in the back. I know I'd never do something like this to her.

But she went ahead and did it to me. I seriously can't believe it.

It occurs to me that I'm actually still kissing Keith and should probably try to focus on that, though to be honest I would rather be curled in a ball on the floor of my closet right now. After about five more minutes of face-smushing discomfort, I realize I'm not quite sure how to bring the whole making-out situation to a close.

Luckily the show ends and everyone boos as the lights come up. Keith mumbles something at my shoes and wanders off to do who-knows-what, so that's solved, I guess. So, what—are we going out now or something? Do I even *want* to go out with Keith Mayhew? Of course, with my luck, Keith will ditch me for Julie Nelson or someone and I'll have to marry Danny Zifner. Or else resign myself to spinsterhood, I suppose. I'll probably end up living with my parents until I'm fifty.

But truth be told, at the moment? I just feel so sad I don't even care.

I go outside and hail a cab, leaving the Traitorous One to figure it out for herself. When I get in the car, I realize I can't even call Em yet, because I know I'll burst into tears as soon as she answers and she won't be able to understand anything I'm saying. And the driver will probably think I'm on drugs.

I succeed in not crying the whole way home.

. . .

After surviving three endless minutes of small talk with my parents, who are pretending they weren't waiting up for me but were just "hanging out" in the kitchen, I finally get to my room and look in the mirror above my dresser.

There I am: Kelsey Finkelstein, a girl who has been kissed and betrayed all in one night. I look a mess; the skin around my mouth is swollen and red. I might as well be wearing a big sign that says, "I just had an uncomfortable makeout session!" I can't believe my parents didn't say anything. I think about washing my face and brushing my teeth, but I just don't feel up to it, so I crawl into bed fully clothed. The tears finally start pouring down my cheeks, and even though I know I'm going to be yelled at for mascara-streaked pillowcases, I don't care.

I am never speaking to Cassidy Gayle Rosenblum again. EVER.

Not even if she came to me on my birthday and offered me my own horse (brown, with white feet and a brown mane) and a lifetime pass to Disneyland and the world's biggest chocolate mousse cake. And her Wii system. And a Blu-ray player. And a million dollars. And an unlimited gift card to Sephora.

Not even if she apologized on her hands and knees and offered to become a nun immediately. In the Alps.

Not even if she were in a horrible accident and was about

to die and all she wanted in her final moments were my forgiveness and an opportunity to touch my hand.

Never.

I suddenly feel completely drained. I'm too exhausted to even put my thoughts together, or cry more, or anything. I squeeze my eyes shut and try to sleep.

15

What seems like a *very* short time later, I am nearly suffocated to death by a heavy weight collapsing on top of my stomach.

"What the eff?!" I screech.

"Mom says you have to get up! It's one in the afternoon and you have to help with Chanukah cards!"

I shove Travis off of me, which is easy to do since she weighs about sixty pounds and I'm madder than I've ever been in my whole life, practically.

"Do *not* come into my room without permission! What is with this family? Has no one ever heard of privacy?"

I wipe under my eyes with the side of my hand and come away with big black streaks. My face feels sore and dry from crying, and my legs are all cramped from sleeping in my jeans. What I want is a long, hot shower and to be left alone forever. What I do *not* want is a brat in my room chattering away about Chanukah cards.

"I'm telling Mom you hit me!"

"Fine, knock yourself out. And close the door behind you!" I'm not in the mood for threats from a nine-year-old, thank you very much.

"And you forgot to take your makeup off. You look like a dead corpse!" she shrieks, slamming the door.

"*All* corpses are dead, dummy!" I holler after her, throwing a pillow at the closed door.

I toss my clothes in a pile on the bathroom floor and turn on the shower. I can't stop reliving the moment when the light hit Cassidy's face and I realized she was kissing my true love for everyone to see. Every time I do, it hurts all over again, but I can't stop torturing myself.

I get in the shower and scrub my face to get the makeup and dried tears off. Not to mention every scrap of Keith Mayhew, kissing stand-in. I can't believe I hooked up with him when I didn't even want to. I'd probably feel worse about that if I didn't feel so bad for myself already. One thing at a time, I guess.

I'm rinsing the shampoo out of my hair when a major thought interrupts my nightmare replay: *Why on God's green earth would Jordan pick Cassidy?!*

I comb conditioner through my hair as I mull this over. Lexi I could understand. I'd still be incredibly upset, but she's gorgeous and perfect, so it's at least logical. Cassidy . . . well, sometimes she can be far too liberal with the eye shadow. And she wears a weird belt that has a skull for a buckle. I mean, hello? We are not biker chicks. And . . .

oh, this one time she ate six bacon and banana sandwiches on a dare. That's just disgusting.

And she is probably a *terrible* kisser.

Unless . . . she's a *great* kisser.

Oh my God. *What if Cassidy is this terrific kisser and Keith was right and I'm awful?*

No. No, no, no, no. This simply cannot be the way this goes down. I rinse off and grab a towel. Clearly the only plan of action is to call Em. She'll know what to do.

Her phone rings four times and goes to voice mail. I call again. Same thing. Em is never away from her phone, so she must be talking to James. I call a third time. Surely she'll realize that this is an emergency.

No answer.

I call JoJo, who is apparently still sleeping, because when I say, "JoJo, I am so upset right now—can you talk?" she replies, "Huglubblnxk?"

Great.

I give up on niceties and shout, "I saw Cassidy making out with Jordan Rothman last night at the Scarves show! What the eff is going *on*?"

That snaps her out of it a bit. "Wait, what? Your Jordan? With Cass?"

"Yes, at the concert. She lied, JoJo—she was planning to go with him the whole time! And I think it's been going on for weeks . . . you didn't know about this, right? You'd tell me?"

"Kels, of course I didn't. I swear!"

I'm so relieved—at least I'm not being deceived by *everyone* I hold near and dear. I guess my only real problem, then, is that I've had my heart ripped out, tossed in a blender, and then poured down the garbage disposal. Glad that's cleared up. I tell JoJo, "You have to find out what's going on. Call her. Text her. Send her a psychic message. Find out what the deal is!"

"Okay, okay, I will, but . . . I have to figure out how to handle this. I mean, this is big. Are you okay?"

"Not really," I say, and I hate that my voice catches. I don't feel like spending any more time crying over a stupid guy and a supposed friend. I take a deep breath. "I just want to know what's going on."

"Okay. Don't freak out—maybe it's a big misunderstanding. Maybe it wasn't even her. Or . . . something. Ugh, boys are the worst. Anyway, I'll call you back." JoJo hangs up.

Now what?

I hate waiting.

I kill about an hour by acting out my imminent confrontation with Cassidy in the bathroom mirror. Then I try calling Em again, but she still isn't picking up her cell. I contemplate calling her house phone, but I'm definitely too traumatized to make small talk with her parents right now.

I continue to mope around the house for the rest of the afternoon, occasionally sending JoJo a friendly text, such as

WTF is going on!?!?!? CALL ME. CALL ME OR I WILL HAVE TO MURDER YOU!!!!!!!!

That evening, I'm eating a PB&J in my room after being banished from the dinner table for point-blank refusing to help with the ridiculous Chanukah cards. As I was storming up the stairs, I heard my mother say, "I don't know, Marvin. Do you think she's doing drugs? Maybe we should take her to see that therapist on your racquetball team . . ." before I slammed my door as hard as possible. Why, I'd like to know, is teenage angst always blamed on drugs instead of totally insensitive parents?

Just as I'm about to go back to the kitchen to stick my head in the oven, my cell rings at last. It's JoJo.

"Finally! What were you doing all this time? Are you trying to give me a second nervous breakdown?"

"Well, I—"

"Never mind, never mind. What did she say? Tell me everything." My devastation has temporarily been replaced by an almost manic need to know exactly what is going on. I feel like, if I have all the information, I can make sense of this whole thing. I don't *want* to know, really . . . but I *need* to know.

"Well, actually . . . I don't think I feel comfortable talking to you about what Cass said," JoJo mumbles hesitatingly. "I just . . . well, you're both my friends. I don't want to get in the middle. I want to stay neutral here."

"What? I'm sorry—what?" I sputter in disbelief.

"I'm staying neutral. I'm sorry—don't be pissed, Kels. I want to help."

"'Staying neutral'? Look, JoJo . . . neutral is stupid. If neutral were a good idea, more people would move to Sweden. Or Switzerland. Or . . . wherever. You can't just . . . come on!" What could Cassidy have said to her? I feel like my life is falling apart. This cannot be happening.

JoJo is still talking about not wanting to take sides when suddenly I have a brilliant idea: I'll call Lexi! Maybe she'll have some insider info, since everyone worships her and probably just blabs all their personal info to her if she says hi to them in the hallway. Armed with a new plan, I quickly tell JoJo not to worry about it, whatever, and hang up.

I scroll to Lexi's number in my phone. I've never called her before, except as part of the soccer phone tree, and even though she's made all those friendly overtures, I still feel a little weird about it. Like I'm asking her out or something.

Well, whatever. This is an emergency situation.

She picks up after two rings and after some generic how-are-you chitchat I get down to business. As nonchalantly as possible, I ask, "So, want to hear something crazy? Guess who was totally hooking up at the Scarves show last night?"

"You?" Lexi guesses.

"Oh, well actually, yeah. Ha." I give her a brief rundown of that disaster.

"Has Keith called you yet?" Lexi asks, which is something I hadn't even stopped to think about in my Cassidy-Jordan frenzy. Am I dissed? Do I care?

I breezily say, "Eh, I'll just see Keith tomorrow at school. It was pretty casual," like I randomly make out with guys in our class all the time or something. Then I add, "Anyway, the big scoop is about Cassidy and Jordan! Can you believe it? Hahahahaha. Ha. Ha?"

Silence on her end. *I knew it!* I think. *She's into him too and now she's furious! We can destroy Cassidy together!*

But then Lexi says, "Really? That's surprising. I mean, Jordan's such a jackass."

Well, that isn't what I expected her to say at *all*. Are we talking about the same Jordan here? Beautiful, blue-eyed Jordan? Jordan, who . . . well, I guess I never stopped to think much about his personality, actually. He's just so hot, it didn't seem to matter.

"Um, what do you mean?" I demand. "Jordan is awesome!"

"Ugh, Kelsey, he's a total loser! He's been hitting on me in a seriously gross way ever since I got here, like grabbing at me in the halls and stuff. I finally told him to cut it the hell out, and now he does this stupid thing where he laughs when he sees me in the hall or pretends to be talking about me. Like I care, right? It's so pathetic and rude. At least in LA guys have manners."

Okay . . . that is pathetic and rude, true. *He was grabbing at her, though?* Moment of pitiful self-loathing: Despite everything, I am still *completely* envious. Grabbing what, exactly? My boobs are way bigger than hers—or Cassidy's, for that matter. Why hadn't he ever tried to grab *them*? Oh my God. Am I really having these thoughts? I need to pull myself together.

Lexi continues, "Anyway, I guess I just thought Cassidy had better taste in guys. Besides, Jordan's been doing it with Lori Soler since, like, mid-October. Didn't you know that? I thought everybody knew that."

Wait. What?!

So, back in seventh grade, a teacher supposedly walked in on a girl giving a very special performance in the music room with this guy who didn't even go to our school. That girl was Lori Soler, and according to the bathroom walls, nothing has changed since.

And now Jordan is hooking up with her? Actually having *sex* with her? First of all, I can't believe people in my grade are seriously having sex. Well, I guess I *can* believe it—I watch TV, for God's sake. But Jordan? What is with this guy? I mean, with *Lori Soler*? Is he that desperate? He could have had *ME*, for crying out loud!

Well. You know what I mean.

Lexi and I chat a bit more about boys and their typical animal behavior and then we hang up. I have a lot to digest, obviously, not to mention a serious dilemma: Can I let my anger at Cassidy prevent me from telling her that she's getting played? Even if she is a cruel, terrible person at the moment, she's still technically one of my best friends.

And I certainly don't want Cassidy to get an STD or something. I have no choice but to eat an entire box of fudge while I think it over, and then watch *Save the Last Dance* for about the eighty-sixth time instead of finishing my homework.

But I can't even concentrate on that. I keep thinking about the whole mess. Can I really not say anything to Cassidy? She needs to know the truth, and from a friend; finding out through the rumor mill might serve her right for dashing my hopes and dreams, but it would be humiliating and awful for her.

But: if Jordan is having sex with Lori Soler, does that mean . . . could that mean that *Cass* is doing it with him too? Which would mean that a) she'd lost her virginity b) to Jordan, who was supposed to be with me, and c) hadn't even *told me*, one of her best friends. And if she obviously cares so little about our friendship in the first place, then why should I bother telling her about Jordan and his filthy love triangle anyway?

But I should tell her. It's the right thing to do. She's still my . . . even though she . . . I couldn't . . .

I must've dozed off, because around ten-thirty I wake up to Travis dancing around in the TV room like a maniac and my mother hollering about the disappearance of all the fudge. I drag myself to my bed, but I can't sleep. All I can think about is Cassidy having sex with Jordan. I mean, have they done it once? A lot of times? Did it hurt? Was it . . . enjoyable? How do they, sort of, arrange themselves, really? Am I actually a bit glad I maybe have a devirginized friend who can tell me how the whole thing actually works in real life and not just how it looks on TV? Assuming I can ever be friends with her again?

It suddenly strikes me as so weird that Cassidy—who last year at this time hadn't even kissed a guy, just like me—might now be on this whole other playing field. I mean, can we even relate to each other anymore? What am I going to say to her? "Oh my God, guess what? I kissed Keith Mayhew for ten minutes and I don't think I liked it!" She'd snootily reply, "Oh, Kelsey, I'd love to talk about your childish games and suchlike, but I have to go to lunch at Pastis with my adult friends who have actual intercourse. Sorry."

And what if lots of other kids are doing it, too? What if *all* of them are? JoJo got to third with some guy who worked at a record store last summer. No idea if she's ever made out with a girl, assuming she does in fact want to. Em hasn't had sex with James yet, but I know she's been thinking about it. *What if I'm the only virgin left in the freshman class?* Is that even normal? I mean, we're only fourteen. Doesn't anyone want to, like, wait for five minutes before having sex all over the place?!

Maybe Lexi is wrong. Just because she has a pierced nose and a perfect body (and hair) doesn't mean she knows *everything*.

16

When I wake up in the morning I have sheet marks all over my face, I look like I just escaped from Shawshank Prison, and I still don't know what to do.

I drag myself to school and sort of float through the morning in a daze. After second period I see Cassidy in the hall. We stare at each other for a sec and then look away, which is so weird. I mean, normally we'd zip right over to each other and start chatting, but now it feels like I don't even know her. And frankly, I don't want to talk to her. She's the one who betrayed *me*, after all!

She finally comes over to me with this fixed look on her face, her jaw tight like it's wired shut or something. She goes, "Well, JoJo told me that you saw us on Saturday night. So . . . I guess it's good that you know. I was trying to figure out how to tell you anyway."

Did she just say "us" to me? Like they're a recognized couple now, and I'm just supposed to go along with that? I can't believe that was her opening line. Doesn't she realize how hurt I am? Did she even think about it for a *second*?

"Oh, really?" I hiss through gritted teeth. "You were try-ing to 'figure it out'? How hard were you working on that, exactly? Because I have to say, I'm not very impressed."

"You know, you can't really be mad at me about this, Kelsey. I mean, it's not like you guys ever hooked up. You barely even ever talk. And—"

"Cassidy, you have known for *years* how I felt about him. And you knew that this was the year I really wanted to try and make it happen now that Jemma's gone—we've talked about it a million times!" I'm fighting to keep my voice down, since people are already glancing with interest in our direction, but it's not easy. "How could you do this to me? You're supposed to be one of my best friends!"

"Kelsey, you can't just, like, *claim* a guy—how is that fair?"

"Fair? Are you serious? I'm talking about our friendship, Cass. Though apparently that doesn't really exist anymore."

"Well, if you're not even going to be reasonable, then maybe it doesn't!"

I stand there gaping at her. She looks at me, still haughty with her chin in the air, but I think I can see it quivering a little bit. I don't know what to say. The bell rings and she walks away, leaving me standing there looking at a row of lockers.

Wow.

At lunch, I head to the caf and take my usual seat at our table with JoJo, but Cassidy is conspicuously missing. I glance around and find her in seconds—sitting with Jordan at a table across the room.

"Really?" I turn to JoJo in disbelief. "Really? She's sitting with him now?"

JoJo follows my gaze and raises an eyebrow at me, but doesn't comment. I guess her whole "neutral" thing is still in effect. Dammit.

"Hey, guys!" Lexi sits down next to me, tossing her lunch on the table and her backpack on the floor. Yay—a non-neutral person I can vent to! Excellent.

"Lex," I begin, "you seriously won't believe what happened after second period today."

"Oh, did you talk to—"

Em walks over with a tray and sits down across from me, since Lexi is in her usual seat. I'm so glad to see her, finally; I still haven't gotten to even tell her about the concert yet, much less ask her advice or tell her about the Lori Soler thing—we've been in different classes all morning.

"Em! I have so much to talk to you about," I say, leaning in. "For starters, don't look now, but my former friend Cassidy has a new boyfriend—an official one, apparently, according to lunchroom seating politics." I guess I'm past depression and into the anger phase. "So where were you last night?"

"I was—"

"And can you believe Cassidy? Wait till you hear what Lexi told me. I'm still totally in—"

"Oh, hello, little freshman girls." It's Julie Nelson, flanked by Ned and one of her other cronies, looming over the table. How does someone that hulking and horrible always manage to sneak up on me so successfully?

Julie stands next to our table for approximately forever, droning on and on about how great she is while nibbling on a protein bar. She's obviously just here to torture me, so I wish she'd just get on with it already.

"You know," she says, "our last game of the season is Thursday. I'm sure you're all coming out to support the team, right? Oh, and Kelsey, you're planning to shock everyone by doing something other than cower inside the net for once, right?" See? I knew it.

"Julie—" I start, but Lexi interrupts me.

"Julie, don't you have anything better to do than bug Kelsey all the time? I mean, at least come up with some new material or something. Seriously."

Ack! What is Lexi doing? Trying to get me killed? I appreciate her support and everything . . . but I really wish she'd show it some other way, like by pushing me into oncoming traffic. I'm racking my brain for words—any words—that might diffuse the situation, when Lexi starts giggling. Then she pokes Julie conspiratorially in the arm, like she didn't just insult her to her face.

I watch, stunned and relieved, as Julie's face goes from fury to incredulity to a . . . smile? And now she's laughing with Lexi. Even Ned is showing signs of life.

Is that some kind of trick they teach in LA, or what?

The bell rings. "See you at the game, ladies," Julie calls, finally heading off with her minions.

"I, uh . . . well," I stammer, "it was really cool of you to stick up for me like that, Lex. I just never know what to say that won't piss her off, you know?"

"Oh, no problem. She really is such a bitch to you, and for no reason! What an idiot." Lexi shrugs, standing up to leave.

Em starts to ask, "Kelsey, are you—"

"So, did you talk to Cassidy or what?" Lexi continues. Oh, right, Cassidy. For a brief moment there, I'd almost forgotten all about her.

I get up, too, turning to toss what's left of my lunch in the trash, pausing for a second when a flash goes off right in my eye. Through the splotchy blobs in my field of vision, I can sort of see that somebody is taking pictures of the cafeteria staff. Maybe it's a gag for the yearbook? Whatever. I catch up to Lexi and follow her into the hall, trying to relay the Cassidy encounter in full with only three minutes till my next class.

I get to Algebra 2 without a second to spare and slip into my seat. Lucky me: Both Cassidy and Keith are in this class. I've passed Keith in the hall today like a hundred times and he hasn't said a word. Cassidy is texting inside her desk—probably to Jordan. Puke.

I suddenly realize that I *still* haven't talked to Em—I just left her sitting at the lunch table! I text her to meet me at my locker during our shared free period, which is right before the end of the day.

A second later, a little envelope symbol pops up with an incoming text. It's a message from Keith, six seats over, and it says: **Hey Kels. Cool time at show. Not 2 B a dick, but not up for comitment rite now. Hop we're cool.**

Well, isn't that the cherry on my sundae.

I'm struck with an intense urge to stand up in the middle of class and say, *Oh, what a terrible shame that you aren't up for "comitment." Guess what? I'm not either. By the way, I got you this dictionary to use for future text-message breakups—hope you like it!*

Yeesh. I can't think of anything to write back that doesn't make me sound like I'm upset, which I'm seriously not—not about this, anyway. So I just look over at Keith and shrug. Nice and noncommittal; he seems to like that, since he gives me a thumbs-up.

Seriously? I can't believe I Frenched that guy.

I don't get a response from Em during the next two classes, but we almost always meet at my locker during a free period anyway, so I head straight there when the bell rings. No Em. I sort through my stuff and chat to some kids in the hallway, but still no Em.

Where *is* she? I'm starting to feel weird, like maybe something is wrong. Could she be sick? I head down the hall to the girls' room, thinking maybe she's in there for some reason, but it's empty.

I finally spot her coming out of the library. I'm so relieved to see her; I don't think I've ever needed her advice on so many topics all at once.

"There you are! I've been looking for you *everywhere*! I feel like it's been a year with how much has happened since we last talked. What's up with your phone? I have to tell you—"

I take a second to gulp some much-needed air.

"Yeah, Kels, I know. I got to hear all about it this morning. From Lexi Bradley, not you."

"What? What do you—"

"Do you know how dumb I felt when she started whispering to me in math all about how you hooked up with Keith and I had no clue what she was talking about?"

"Em, I—"

"I can't believe you told her about your first kiss and not me. I thought *I* was your best friend!"

"Em, you *are*! I tried to—"

"And then I find out about Cass and Jordan from JoJo at lunch while Lexi is busy playing your bodyguard with Julie Nelson. What's going on?"

I'm so surprised, I can't even formulate a thought. What is Em so upset about? I'm about to explain that I tried to call her last night when Lexi runs up. We turn around and she squeals, "Hey, guys! Oh, Em, I forgot to tell you, I love your hair like that!" She grabs my arm. "Kelsey, you'll never guess what happened; two different guys asked me to the winter formal today—can you believe that?"

"Of course I can," I say. "I'm sure ten more will have asked you by Friday."

"Yeah, right, but thanks," Lexi goes on. "Anyway, you have to help me decide who to go with on the way to soccer, and I only have a few weeks to get a dress . . ."

I turn back, but Em has been swallowed up by the crowd. Lexi keeps chattering away as we head to the locker room to change for practice. I guess I'll have to call Em the second I get home and straighten this out. But she's Em, so I know she'll understand. She has to.

17

I get home after another horrendous practice (countdown: three days till the last game and the glorious end of the season) and head straight to the kitchen, looking for peace and quiet and maybe some nice, soothing candy. After tossing my backpack and puffy coat and kicking off my Pumas toward the stairs, I head for the fridge to grab some juice. As I reach to get a glass out of the cabinet, suddenly my foot is soaking wet. What the—? I look down and realize I've stepped directly in a bowl of water, which for some reason is on the floor. Next to it is another bowl that appears to be full of Cracklin' Oat Bran cereal. Huh. Interesting.

I'm mopping up the water with paper towels (after peeling my sock off, ick) when I realize the bowls must be for Travis's new pal, Nancy the Cat. As a reward for her great accomplishments in the fourth grade, i.e., spelling her name correctly (does anyone care that my life is in shambles and I could actually *use* some cheering up?), Travis was allowed to take in the cat that's been loitering in our backyard for the last week or so. I've only been begging for a dog for about a thousand years, but apparently I'm not responsible enough to have one and my mother doesn't want to "get stuck walking the damned thing at three in the morning because Kelsey didn't feel like it." Is that any way to talk about a poor defenseless dog? Or a poor defenseless daughter, for that matter?

My mother, the great animal lover, took Nancy the Cat to the vet and spent my entire college fund getting it shots and toys and food and a carrier and who knows what else. I'll tell you this much: When Travis bails on this little project, I am not going to clean the litter box. No way.

I'm so glad that I can return home from school and literally step in yet another reminder of how perfect Travis's life is while mine is a garbage heap swarming with flies.

I run up to my room, furious, damp, and upset. I put on my comfiest pj pants and a hoodie and grab my phone to call Em. She doesn't pick up. What is going *on*? I try again, and leave a message this time, which I usually never even bother to do.

I curl up in my desk chair to spin around and think. I mean, forget Travis and her cat—that's a mere annoyance, really. Ditto soccer, which is almost over at last. And forget Jordan, who is clearly an idiot that I've wasted *years* liking. Keith obviously gets filed under *W* for "Whatever." But the stuff with Cassidy . . . and especially Em, who has never been upset with me before and is, frankly, totally unjustified in this case . . . I mean, I never put Lexi before her—not even once. And anyway, Em is the one who encouraged me to be friends with Lexi in the first place! I just don't know what to do at all.

My mother yells up the stairs something insane about a sock in the sink and wanting me to set the table for dinner and empty the dishwasher. What gives? Can I have two *seconds* to be upset in this stupid house?!

After continued and increasingly angry directives, I sense being grounded may be imminent, which would really put a damper on winter break. I heave a great sigh and go back downstairs, where my mother is doing the crossword puzzle.

"You know, if emptying the dishwasher is soooo important, why didn't *you* do it instead of sitting there doing a crossword puzzle?" I inquire—quite reasonably, I think.

Big mistake. This sets her off on a tirade. Will I never learn?

And then the weirdest thing happens. Maybe it's her shrill, endlessly irritating voice or just the fact that my life is a mess, but I burst into tears. Even as it's happening I'm surprised, though I guess after the last couple of months this is sort of becoming routine. Thanks, hormones.

Anyway, Mom is *really* surprised. And somehow I find myself telling her all about Cass and Jordan and Em (I do not mention Keith for fear she'll overreact and drag me to a gynecologist or something) and she actually really listens. Puts down the newspaper and everything.

Once I get it all out, I actually feel a lot better. She doesn't have any killer advice other than to follow my instincts, but just having her listen really helps. I wipe my face with the sleeve of my hoodie, and Mom actually manages to restrain herself from making a comment about it.

Then she says, "I'll tell you this much, honey: Even if Cassidy *is* experimenting sexually"—*GAG!*—"she is probably one of the few. Everyone always thinks the whole freshman class is getting it on"—*vomit, seriously*—"but then senior year you find out it was three people and a lot of imagination. Otherwise *20/20* would be doing a show about it."

That makes me feel even better still, believe it or not. Until she makes me empty the dishwasher and set the table, despite my obvious need to go back upstairs and do nothing.

There is seriously no way I'm not adopted.

18

The next few days at school I feel like a rat in a maze, only I'm trying to avoid the various cheeses scattered around it. Cass, around the corner! Julie, lurking in the shadows! Hurt glances from Em! Jordan! Lori! Keith! Gaaaaah! I've never looked forward to taking exams before, but at least they're a distraction.

On my way to lunch on Thursday, I finally stake out Em's locker. It's been four days since we've even had a real conversation—she still isn't responding to my calls or texts. At lunch she's been either really late or only spoken in monosyllables. JoJo of course refuses to comment, and I obviously can't talk to Cass about it. I sort of can't believe Em's acting this way; it just seems so unlike her. To not even give me a chance to explain? Something else must be going on, and I'm going to find out what it is.

I feel a tap on my shoulder and turn around expectantly, but it isn't Em. It's Lexi. Argh. She has Spider Sense for bad timing. Maybe that's her fatal flaw?

She says, "Hey, are you waiting for Em? I'm sorry I spilled the beans about Keith the other day, but I just figured you'd already—"

"Yeah, no, don't worry about it. No big deal."

"So, anyway, remember last week at lunch when I was talking about maybe going to a meeting for *The Reflector* or something, and you said you'd come with me? I was thinking I'd really actually like to do it. So, do you think you'd still be up for it?"

"Yeah, of course I will," I say, bending down to adjust my right knee-high boot but really trying to surreptitiously peer around the corner to see if Em is coming. I straighten up. "Listen, Lex, do you think I could meet you in the caf? I kind of need to talk to Em alone for a sec. We've been missing each other a bit lately, and, uh . . ."

"No problem. I totally get it. I'll see you there. And thanks!" A popular sophomore coming down the hall rushes over to Lexi and starts gushing about the winter formal, and off they go.

Okay, that was easy. But now what? I check my watch—it's fifteen minutes into lunch. Would Em have gone straight to the caf without stopping to drop off her books? This is absurd, like I'm in a bad spy movie. I decide to case the library instead. As I walk past the home ec lab, I see movement through the glass panel in the door. I stop to look, just in case Em decided to whip up a batch of snickerdoodles.

Instead, I see Jordan and Lori Soler, groping each other next to the sewing machines.

HOLY CRAP.

I back away in the direction I came from, and there's Em at her locker. I rush over before she can escape.

"Were you waiting for me to leave so you could go to your locker?" I blurt out. Perhaps not my best intro, but at least we're talking.

Em looks at the floor. "I don't know. Maybe."

"Em. Seriously. What is going on with you? What did I do?"

"Nothing. Forget about it." She's still not really looking at me but chipping the paint off the locker next to hers.

"I'm not going to forget about it. You're my best friend and you're not talking to me and I don't know what I did. You're obviously upset about something, but I have so much to tell you and—oh my God, literally one minute ago I saw something completely nuts and I don't know what to—"

"Why don't you tell Lexi about it, then?" Em snaps, finally looking up at me.

"Is that really what this is about? Em, I've tried to call you a million times since the concert—and first, before anyone else! And you didn't pick up the phone. I just don't understand what's going on—why are you so mad at me?"

Em goes back to chipping the paint for a second. Then

she says in a rush, "I just feel like—I mean, you didn't even tell me about kissing Keith. We haven't hung out just the two of us in ages. You were busy with soccer for all of fall and now you're always talking to Lexi and . . . I don't know. I just miss you."

"Em," I say, trying not to get upset. "I miss you too—why do you think I've been stalking you all over school trying to figure out what's going on? I mean, yeah, soccer takes up a lot of my time, but it hasn't exactly been a joyride. And I *have* been spending some time with Lexi . . . but that doesn't mean you aren't still my best, *best* friend. I don't know why you don't believe me, but I call you first no matter what! For all of those things you mentioned—really! But you've been super caught up with James, and . . ."

A tear rolls down Em's cheek.

"Em, what is going *on*?" She wipes at her face as the tears come faster, and people are starting to look at us. I know how much Em hates to be the center of attention, so I quickly grab her books from her and steer her toward the girls' bathroom. Once we get inside, she totally falls apart, sobbing.

"James br-broke up with me," she wails, sputtering through her tears. "And I didn't think you'd c-care because you were only h-h-hanging out with Lexi and I just miss him so much and I feel like s-such a stupid girl about the whole, the whole th-thing . . ."

Oh, no. Poor Em. I feel like the worst friend on the

planet; here I've been mooning around about my imaginary boyfriend when her actual one turned out to be an idiot. I give her a huge hug.

"When did this happen? Have you been keeping it to yourself this whole time? Why didn't you just tell me?"

"Su-Sunday," Em gulps, trying to calm down. Her face is all red and splotchy, so I get her some wet paper towels from the sink. "I know you were trying to call me, but I c-couldn't even talk and then when Lexi told me the next day about—"

"No, I get it. I totally get it," I say. "Boys! Do you realize a couple of stupid guys made us be in the first fight we've ever had? What the eff? We should just become lesbians."

Em smiles a tiny smile, which is encouraging.

"I just—you know," she says, speaking normally again, "you always hear about how in high school people change or . . . change their friend groups and . . . I thought maybe you wanted to be best friends with Lexi and it was too late to tell you about James . . . I don't know. It sounds so dumb."

"It's not dumb. I mean, it would be *very* dumb if it were true. But Em, it's not true. I do like Lexi, but . . . come on. She's no Em Gale!"

Em laughs. A few girls trickle in, and I realize lunch is going to end in a few minutes. Em goes over to the mirror and pulls her hair back. "I look awful," she says. "Do you have a compact?"

"You look terrific!" I lie, reaching into my backpack for

my compact. "Stupid James. That guy is dead to me. Do you hear me? He's DEAD TO ME!" Em laughs again. I'm so relieved to have straightened everything out with Em; it's like a massive weight has been lifted off my shoulders.

I guess I'm not the only one who's been feeling overwhelmed this year, but I'm so used to being the one whose life always falls apart, it never occurred to me that maybe Em's could, too.

"Listen," I say as we walk out together with linked arms, "I need your advice. I've been *needing* your advice—it's major." I tell her all about the Cassidy-Jordan-Lori situation as fast as I can. She thinks for a sec.

Em replies, "I don't want to get between you guys, but you know I think it was really lame of Cassidy to lie about this. I mean, she knew how you felt."

"I know, right?!" I interject forcefully. I'm so glad someone besides me has pointed out this very significant fact. "I mean, what the hell? Anyway, I'm totally over him. Obviously."

"Obviously," she agrees, and thinks some more. "I think the right thing to do is to tell her. But . . . Cass might not believe you. Because she knows how much you like—liked—Jordan, and how pissed you are at her. And upset. She might think you made it up to hurt her as much as she hurt you. So, basically, I have no idea what you should do."

I shake my fist at her jokingly. "I'm so glad we made up

so you could give me the most useless advice ever. What am I supposed to do now?"

Em scrunches her face up and shrugs. "I dunno, Kels," she says. "But you'll figure it out. You always do." The bell rings. Before we part ways, I give her another big hug.

"I'm really sorry about James, Em. He doesn't deserve you. Honestly."

Em smiles weakly. "Thanks," she whispers. "I'm sorry I shut you out. I'll see you at your soccer game tonight, okay?"

Oh, right. The last game.

19

I look out over the darkening field to the bleachers, where a smattering of very cold parents and friends are watching the last girls' JV soccer game of the year. And guess what? We're winning.

Of course, that could be because the team we're playing is incredibly bad at a couple of minor things, such as kicking and running. It's almost insulting that we're playing them, actually, because except for my consistently lousy performance as goalie, our team is pretty good. But the important thing is, in just a few minutes, the most miserable soccer season of my life will be over. *Over!*

I can see Em and JoJo with a few of our other friends in the stands, stamping their feet to stay warm. Ana has the ball at the moment, and she passes to Steli, who takes it down the field and scores again. Yay for us. So, can we go home now?

Please?

My wish is finally granted when the clock runs out, and

after we do the "good game" high fives with the other team, we huddle around Coach Cantwell and Julie.

"Great way to end the season, ladies!" the coach effuses. "Now, I know we didn't place as high regionally as we have in previous years, but I want to thank all of you for your good sportsmanship blah blah blah . . ."

As Coach Cantwell drones on and on, Lexi and I roll our eyes at each other. I can't wait to get this disgusting goalie armor off and shower for about a week.

". . . like to thank Julie for being a terrific captain! And lastly, don't forget that the sports awards assembly will be blah blah blah . . ."

Finally she wraps it up and I practically sprint over to my friends in the bleachers. "We have to get some pizza immediately," I gasp. "I think I'm dying of malnutrition."

"I'm not going to a public place with you smelling like that," JoJo replies, wrinkling her nose. "You barely even moved the whole game! How can you smell so horrible?"

"JoJo!" Em scolds her. "Don't be a jerk."

"Oh, come on. I'm only saying what you're thinking. Kelsey, you smell like a . . . like a foot. A diseased foot."

"Gee, thanks, JoJo." I hold my nasty padded goalie shirt away from myself. "Ugh, I can't wait to get this stupid uniform off. Listen, I'm going to run in and toss this thing in my gym locker. Meet me by the front doors, okay?"

"Okay, but hurry. It's cold!"

I head inside the locker room and wrestle the goalie garb off. It does smell disgusting. I really should just light it on fire, for all the good it's done me this year. I pull on my regular clothes and text Em that I'm coming. Then I text Lexi and ask her to save us all seats at Antonio's, since that's where everyone is heading.

It's faster to go back outside than through the building to get to the front doors, so I circle back around the field, where the guys' varsity team is playing. I see Cassidy standing near our team's goal, watching Jordan play. I have to admit, he looks really good out there. Then I remember that he is an imbecile. And even though the last thing I want to do right now is talk to her at all, I absolutely have to tell Cass about Lori Soler.

I decide it's better to just get it over with, so I go over and clear my throat. "Um, can I talk to you for a second? I really need to tell you something."

"Did you come to apologize?"

"Uh, no. What would *I* be apologizing for?!"

"Well, if you don't know, I'm not going to explain it to you. Anyway, I'm watching my boyfriend right now. Can't it wait?"

Well, that's nice. This is off to an excellent start.

"Cass. It's *important*. Seriously."

She finally looks at me and heaves a big dramatic sigh. "Okay, what? Are you still mad that I'm going out with

Jordan? I'm not going to let you make me feel bad, because I didn't do anything wrong."

"Cassidy, this isn't about that. Although, since you asked, yes, I'm really pissed at you. But I still think it's my responsibility as a friend to tell you that . . . um . . . well, that Jordan isn't who you think he is."

She's blinks at me with wide "oh, you poor deluded soul" eyes. Then she says, "Kelsey, you don't know anything *about* Jordan. That's sort of the whole point, isn't it?"

See, this is not making me want to be a good, kind, and caring friend. But I think about what I saw in the home ec room and I know that, despite everything, I must persevere.

"Cass," I say. "Jordan is . . . okay, um, as your *friend*, I thought I should tell you that Jordan is sleeping with Lori Soler behind your back and everyone knows about it but you. And I think you need to, uh, confront . . ."

I sort of run out of steam at this point, partly because I don't really know what she should do, and partly because Cassidy is looking at me like I just blew up her house with her entire family inside.

I decide this is a bad time to ask if she's still a virgin.

Through her teeth, she growls, *"You. Are. Pathetic."* She turns on her heel and stomps to the other side of the field, not looking back.

Okay, then. That went well.

When I finally get back to JoJo and Em, they are practically Popsicles.

"Sorry, sorry! I had to stop and have an unbelievably awkward conversation with Cassidy, which I'm pretty sure ended our friendship permanently. Who knew that would take so long?"

"Oh, nooooo!" Em exclaims, breathing into her hands for warmth as we walk. "She didn't believe you about Lori?"

"Not so much, no. And not only didn't she believe me, but now I think she actually hates me! Which is incredibly ironic, if you want my opinion."

"Come on," JoJo says, always the optimist, "you guys are just having a moment. Like when my dad hit his second drummer in the head with a guitar and they didn't speak for, like, six years. It'll blow over."

"Thanks, JoJo. That's . . . very reassuring. But honestly? I think I'm done. I mean, hello? She betrayed *me*. And I still tried to be a good friend! And what do I get? Nothing!"

"Kels, you know I decided to stay—"

"I know, I know—you're staying neutral. Everyone is neutral. Well, then, you guys can buy me some pizza. Because guess what?"

"What?" Em opens the door to Antonio's and a delicious wave of cheese and warm bread hits us.

"I'm not a goalie anymore! I'm free! The nightmare is over!"

20

Winter break slides by in a blur of holiday shopping with my friends, reminding Lexi that she could wear a garbage bag and still look amazing at the upcoming winter formal, sleeping in, consoling Em when James doesn't respond to her e-mails, wondering what is happening in the Cassidy-Jordan-Lori love triangle, being harassed by my parents for not helping them clean out the basement, and eating way too much pie. Before I even blink, school is upon me again. How does that happen? Infuriating.

On the morning of our first day back at school, I'm walking down the hall to class when I see a new sheet on the activities board. It's audition sign-ups for the spring musical.

Auditions are going to be held in two weeks, and the show is *Fiddler on the Roof*. Which is a pretty uninspired and stodgy choice, if you ask me. What, does the costume department have a giant pile of head kerchiefs lying around and that's what they based their decision on? I remember watching the movie at Hebrew school in, like, fifth grade, and I was not impressed. I mean, not to disrespect my people, but what's so interesting about a bunch of Jews dancing around with bottles on their heads?

I take a closer look at the flyer. There's only one name on it so far—NED GARMAN, in block letters. Evil Cassidy will be all about this; she's been waiting for the spring musical since day one. The wheels in my head start turning in a most devilish manner. What if . . . what if I audition, too? And what if I get a part and she doesn't? That would definitely give her a tiny taste of the pain she's caused me this year. Which would totally serve her right.

Oh, petty revenge! Don't knock it till you try it.

But do I even want to be *in* a play? Could I actually get cast? I've never been in one that wasn't enforced as part of a ridiculous school requirement, i.e., dressing up as a ladybug and reciting "Ladybug, Ladybug, Fly Away Home" during a second-grade assembly. (I was excellent, if I do say so myself—it was an extremely moving performance.)

What if I've been sitting on this untapped well of theatrical talent for years and didn't even know it? What if said talent is just waiting to be unleashed amid a group of singing, melancholy Jewish villagers? I mean, I *can* sing—at least in the shower. I know I'm not tone deaf, since I wasn't one of the kids asked to lip-sync in elementary school choir.

So maybe I could get a part as one of the daughters or something. Of course, it's more likely that only the upperclassmen will get parts—seriously, high school is the most ageist place in the universe. But what if I auditioned and got a lead role, out of nowhere, and all the drama geeks—including their oh-so-cool leader, Ned Garman—would be like, *Really? Kelsey Finkelstein?*

Maybe JoJo and Em will audition, too, and we can all be in it together. That would be so fun! The longer I stand here thinking about it, the better this idea sounds. The only real cons I can come up with are that, one, being in a show with Cass would be even more awkward than just being at school with her (not to mention sharing a couple of best friends), and two, I don't know any songs from musicals to try out with except "Oh, What a Beautiful Morning" from *Oklahoma*. Which I don't think would do anything so much as annoy the hell out of Mr. Zinner, the drama teacher (whom I've never spoken to but have seen going in and out of the theater building. One word: *combover*).

The bell rings, and I quickly scribble my name on the list. Why not? I can always change my mind.

By the end of the next day, I notice the sign-up sheet for the play has filled up pretty substantially. Cassidy's name is on there, of course, and a lot of people I don't know at all. The auditions aren't far off, so if I'm going to do this thing, I guess I'd better figure out my strategy.

I grab Em, who I convinced to try out as well to distract from her broken heart, and we head over to the school library. The plan is to get sheet music for something we can sing at our auditions. It turns out there are about ten thousand musical scores back there, most of them dog-eared and marked up. Who knew our school was so well stocked with that sort of thing?

Apparently I'm not the only one with the brilliant idea to try the library; I hear some low talking and peer through a bookcase to the other side of the section. There's a group of kids sitting at a round table, surrounded by pages and pages of music, and of course Ned is holding court—blissfully without Julie for once.

Ned drones on while pointing to different books, and the other kids are listening to him like he's the Dalai Lama. "Blah blah blah choosing your song," he says. "Blah blah your soul, blah blah show your range blah blah unsung musicals blah blah out of the box."

Em and I start leafing through the books on our side of the shelves. I whisper, "Gee willikers, I sure hope something 'out of the box' will reach out and grab me."

Em giggles and peeks through at Ned's group again. "Hey, are they holding hands? Is it a prayer group or something?"

I glance over, and Ned and his followers are indeed holding hands in a circle around the table with their eyes closed.

"You better not have convinced me to be in some kind of cult, Kels!"

"Yeah, because I really want to join a cult. That's priority number one for me, Em, didn't I mention that?"

"You know, Cassidy could probably help us pick—"

"Don't start that again." Em has been dropping little you-guys-should-make-up hints like this since Cass and I had our last exchange at the soccer game—which was weeks ago now. "Look, I know it's weird with us not being friends, but I'm not the one who—"

"SHHHHHHHHH!"

Yikes. A very intense-looking girl wearing even more eyeliner than Ned is pressing her face right up against the space in the bookcase and glaring at us. She must be a very good actress, because I am totally scared. Em and I quickly grab our stuff, stifling nervous laughter, and hightail it out of there.

That night, I head to my room to do some homework after dinner, and the first book I pull out is a score from the library. Oops. Guess I forgot to actually check it out when Em and I were running for our lives from the theater kids. It's for a show called *Wicked*, which I've never seen but I know has something to do with *The Wizard of Oz*.

I thumb through it and it looks pretty good to me—I mean, I don't know anything about musicals, so it might as well be this one. At least I've heard of it.

I go downstairs and plunk out a few songs on the piano with one finger. Good thing I had all those piano lessons, huh? Ha. I kind of like this one song, "Defying Gravity," which appears to be the big showstopper. I guess I should see if I can find someone singing it on YouTube for comparison, but it seems really easy to sing and the words aren't hard to remember.

So I guess that's that.

Assuming I decide to go through with the audition, of course.

21

On Friday, three days later, the crack newspaper photographer strikes yet again. I'm in study hall when Ana Blau passes a copy of the new *Reflector* to me. It's open to the features section. A picture in the middle of the page is circled with pink highlighter and underneath is written *Is this YOU?!?!*

It's a story about the cafeteria workers. The picture shows five of them standing together, smiling . . . and me. Standing slightly apart, and facing a bit sideways, but definitely in line with the group. Also, I'm not actually looking at the camera, which makes me look like there is something seriously wrong with my face.

I suddenly realize that this must have been the source of the giant flash when I was leaving the caf the day Lexi stood up to Julie for me. Ugh—that's the thing about school papers. All the "news" is a month old, so you can't even put horrendous moments in history behind you. Not if some kid decides to write a story about them, anyway.

I look closely at the outfit I'm wearing in the picture.

Dark skinny jeans and a white long-sleeved T-shirt under a kelly green V-neck sweater. The cafeteria staff wear black pants and blue V-neck vests over white collared shirts, but in the black-and-white photo, if you just glance quickly at it . . . I totally look like a member of the caf staff. (Who ripped off her hairnet on her way to execute an emergency inspection of a vat of creamed corn or something. Ostensibly with her one good eye.)

Well, isn't that a *delight*.

I look over at Ana and mime shooting myself in the head. She makes a WTF face at me, then immediately goes for her phone. Excellent. Within minutes, my whole grade will think that I moonlight as a mashed potato scooper.

This is the last straw—Staff Photographer, I am coming for you. And it's not going to be pretty.

I text Lexi to meet me at the *Reflector* office the second lunch starts. I have a feeling that putting in an appearance at the caf today isn't in my best interest—unless I feel like serving meat loaf to hysterically laughing classmates. Based on the looks I'm getting in the hall between classes, I have a feeling a few other people saw this month's Features section as well.

Lexi is waiting for me, leaning casually up against the door frame. "Hey, Kels!" she says. "Thanks so much for offering to come with me. I know it's silly to be nervous, but—"

"Oh, no problem! Let's go." I practically yank her arm

off dragging her through the door. And . . . no one is inside. It's just a classroom with a bunch of computers on a long table and a Xerox machine in the corner. On the walls are bulletin boards with all kinds of lists on them, probably of upcoming stories or whatever. I'm amazed there isn't one that says "Destructive Candids of Kelsey Finkelstein Earmarked for Future Use."

But on the wall I see a contact list. Excellent. I'll just find out who the photographer that took those pictures is, and—

"Hey, can I help you guys with something?"

I whirl around, startled. In the doorway is a guy I don't remember seeing at school before. He's definitely not a freshman. He's definitely not ugly. He's—

"Oh, hiiiii," Lexi purrs, slinking over to him. For someone who was so nervous about looking like a dork, she seems to have recovered extremely well. "I'm Lexi Bradley. I was wondering about writing for the paper?" She cocks her head to the side coquettishly and extends her hand. He shakes it, though I'm pretty sure he'd much rather give her a full-body search.

"Well, we're always looking for new writers," he says warmly. His eyes are very dark, and they crinkle at the corners when he smiles. I'd probably find that adorable if I weren't so furious about the K. Finkelstein Series of Embarrassing Selective Photography. "You need to talk to Kate, the editor in chief. I can give you her e-mail, um . . .

lemme just grab a piece of paper." He takes a piece of blank paper out of the copy machine and scribbles some stuff on it. Then he glances over at me. "Are you a writer, too?" he asks.

"What? No. No, I'm here to file a complaint." I slam the side of my hand down on the desk, much harder than I had intended. Now I've both made a loud noise *and* hurt my hand. I decide to pretend it didn't happen and move on. I stealthily tuck my injured hand behind my back. "So, yes. I want to file a complaint and request that, um . . ."

I grind to a halt because the guy is biting his lip like he's trying not to laugh. Also adorable, and even more infuriating. "Oh. Okay," he says. "Well, I'm the only one here at the moment, so . . . I guess you can, um, file it with me? I'm—"

"She's looking for whoever takes the pictures," Lexi jumps in helpfully. She winks at me from behind the guy's back and then sidles up next to him. Okay, yes, he is *very* cute. But whose side is she on here, anyway?

"Oh. Well, we don't really have a budget for camera equipment, so people just submit stuff. But . . . why, what happened?"

"Well, for some reason I keep ending up in these extremely unflat—"

"Do you want some ice for that?" The guy nods in the direction of my hand, which does look a bit red, actually. Dammit.

"No, thank you. I want to—"

"Because I could get you some from the teachers' lounge next door. I wouldn't want you to have to file a second complaint for acquiring an injury in the newspaper office." He grins teasingly, his eyes crinkling up at the corners again.

This guy is totally making fun of me! I think. *Or maybe he's flirting with me? Agh, why is it so hard to tell?*

I think I hate him.

"I want to find out who submitted certain pictures of me, then," I tell him. "How many people do you have doing that? Isn't there a . . . record? I mean, I don't know why I'd be singled out, but they're extremely horrible and you guys need to check things a little more carefully from now on! I mean, this is the newspaper, right? Isn't fact-checking supposed to be a big deal around here?" Why did I think this was a good idea, again? I give Lexi a look, like, *Help, please.*

"Yeah, like this picture today," Lexi offers, picking up a copy of the new edition from one of the desks and opening it to the features section. *Oh, no.* Can we not employ hideous visual aids, please? "See this? Kelsey doesn't work for the caf staff. She isn't even wearing a vest!"

He looks at the picture, and I think his head might actually explode from trying to hold his laughter in.

"Wow." He takes the picture and looks at it closely, and then over at me. "That is . . . definitely a terrible oversight. I'm sure that, uh, Kate will feel really bad about this—she does the final check of everything before we go to print.

But you know, we don't have a whole lot of time to get everything together for each issue. We're a pretty small staff. And the file with the JPEGs is kind of a mess. It's the last thing that gets done when we're laying out the issue—you know, we just kind of grab stuff. I mean, if you wanted to come back, maybe you could sift through them all and try to figure out who brought the ones of you in? It might take a while, though."

Oh, yeah, sure. Let's set up my return appointment right now. Can't wait.

"If it makes you feel better," he continues, "I wouldn't have known this was you. Seriously." And . . . cue eye crinkling.

I think I've amused this guy enough for one day. Time to wrap it up.

"Great, well, could you just ask Kate or whoever to not put in any more pictures with me in the background? You'll have Lexi on your staff now, so hopefully she can, you know, help with that. Fact-checking and picture, um, cropping." *Terrific, Kelsey. Anything else you'd like to add while you're at your most eloquent?*

I start moving toward the door, which seems like the best course of action. The guy, still smiling, turns on one of the computers and takes a folder out of his messenger bag. "Right. Well, I'll definitely pass on your message . . ."

"Kelsey," Lexi offers. "Kelsey Finkelstein. And I'm Lexi."

"Got it. Kelsey and Lexi. School paper enthusiasts."

"What? No, not enthusiasts," I correct him hastily. "Beleaguered, disgruntled—"

"You've got a pretty impressive vocabulary for a freshman," he interrupts. "You sure you don't want to write for the paper?"

Okay, he's definitely making fun of me. Right?

"Just please tell her about the pictures, okay? Thanks. So, Lexi, let's . . . Lex, we're leaving now. Hello?"

I finally manage to drag Lexi off her perch on the corner of the computer table, where both she and Mr. Smiley Eyes are admiring her hair. Once we're out of earshot, she says, "Kels. That guy is *so hot.* And he thinks you're really smart. Come on, work on the paper with me! Musicals are lame."

"That guy thinks *he* is really smart. And how did he know I was a freshman, anyway?" I grumble, rubbing my wounded hand. It still hurts.

"Um, maybe he's seen, uh . . ."

"Oh, don't bother. I might as well be wearing a sign."

Lexi giggles, looking at the sheet of paper the guy gave her. "Oh, I totally know who Kate is—Molly Izzo's older sister."

"Seriously? Damn! I could've just asked *her* about the pictures instead of taking the 'Kelsey is a nutbar' show to the newspaper office."

"Yeah, but it's such a good show," Lexi quips. I flick her

on the arm. "Besides, I needed your moral support! And anyway, then we wouldn't have met . . . huh. What was that guy's name, anyway?"

Before I can respond, Cassidy shoves past us, her arms full of sheet music books. "Excuse me! Oh, sorry, *Lexi*." She doesn't meet my eye, not that I want to meet hers. But when did she become such a bitch?

Lexi gives me a sympathetic look. "It's not your fault, Kels. She'll find out about Jordan for herself and then you'll make up."

"Ha! Who says I even want to make up with her, anyway?" I scoff. "And I'll tell you something else: Musicals might be lame, but I'm auditioning for this one. And I'm gonna *kill* it."

22

The second I get home from school, I grab the *Wicked* score, head to the living room, and plunk out my song on the piano. Not bad, if I do say so myself. But after about fifteen very intense minutes of rehearsal, I get bored and decide to head over to JoJo's for the night.

I get to JoJo's around seven. She and her parents just finished eating, and of course JoJo is having a glass of wine, so I figure I'll have one, too. It must be so weird having parents who don't have any rules. I mean, awesome, but . . . weird.

After her parents go upstairs, we lounge around in the living room, flipping through channels. I take a sip from the bottle of Skyy vodka JoJo brought from the kitchen—it's not so bad on its own, actually. The taste reminds me of how nail polish remover smells, which I've always sort of liked. Besides, I'm starting to feel buzzed.

JoJo is sprawled in front of the TV, thumbing through DVDs. She asks, "Do you want to watch something funny or serious?"

"Whatever, I don't care."

"We could watch my parents' pornos. They're *hilarious*."

I practically choke on a mouthful of vodka. "Um, thanks, but I'd rather just chew my arm off. How about a nice slasher film instead?"

"Suit yourself . . . but you never know, Kelsey, you might learn something. Which could come in handy next time you and Keith—"

"Okay—that will be all, thank you," I interrupt hurriedly. "As you may recall, he's not ready for a 'comitment.' Thank God—I have enough to deal with as it is." Ugh. Keith Mayhew. That's an error in judgment I won't be making twice. I decide to swiftly change the subject.

"So," I say slyly. "How's my former friend Cassidy doing, anyway? I shared a *lovely* moment with her in the hall today. . . ."

JoJo gives me her patented raised eyebrow. "Kelsey, I'm not having a Cass-bashing session."

"I didn't say anything mean!" I protest. "I just asked how she was!"

JoJo chugs a few swallows of vodka, then says, "She's okay. Yes, she's still dating Jordan, and no, she doesn't believe you about Lori Soler."

"Didn't you *tell* her it was true?"

"Well, I didn't see them together like you did . . . and anyway, I don't want her to be pissed off at me, too. She asked him about it and he said it was a lie. So . . . she be-lieves him. But I think she feels bad about what went down with you guys," JoJo explains.

Ah, excellent. The wonderful, wonderful vodka is loos-ening JoJo's previously impenetrable tongue. I push on. "Please. If she feels so bad about it, how come she parades around school acting like I don't even exist? It's beyond childish."

"Childish? Like . . . trying out for a play you couldn't care less about just to try and make her feel bad?"

"Um, that is a totally different situation! And I do so care about the play. I told you months ago, this is the year I'm going to mark up . . . I mean, *make* a mark! I didn't say it *had* to be through soccer, you know. I've been seerearching—researching—wait, hang on." I take a swig from the bottle and pass it back to JoJo. Man, that stuff burns the throat.

"Look, you can't *totally* blame Cassidy," JoJo says. "I mean, yes, she was a jerk for lying about Jordan. But why didn't you make a move on him yourself? You're hot! You're awesome! You could've just gone for it. So . . . what gives?"

"JoJo, you have made some excellent points, especially the part about how Cassidy was a jerk, though I think, really, I'd classify her more specifically as a—"

"Don't make me switch back to my neutral status!" she warns, lifting that eyebrow again.

Arrrgh. Must proceed with caution. "Fine. So, what was I supposed to *do*? It's not like I was going to walk up to him in the hall and be like, 'Hi, Jordan, feel like making out today?'"

"That's probably what Cassidy did." JoJo giggles. "You *should've* done that. I bet he'd've said *'Hells yeah!'* and given you the J. Rothman special. Maybe you could try it on someone else. Maybe a certain cute newspaper guy? Lexi told me during last period that some dude was totally flirting with you."

"Come on, get real." Now I'm starting to get the alcohol spins—just the early stages, when they feel really good. Tra la la laaaaaa . . .

"*You* get real!"

"*You* get real *first*!" I scoff. "Blech. Boys are stupid."

"You don't have to tell me," she agrees. "Frankly, I don't know why you bother with them at all."

I don't say anything, wondering if maybe she'll finally expand on the topic. I ready myself to be reassuring and enthusiastic about her sexual awakening . . . but instead she pulls out her battered Connect Four game from under the TV and starts setting it up.

Am I imagining this whole gay thing? And where is that vodka, anyway?

Why, oh, why is Connect Four so fun when you're drunk?

And hey—why is Lexi telling people that that guy was flirting with me? He so wasn't! He was just enjoying the sound of his own voice, that's all.

He was cute, though. For an egomaniac, that is.

Five games later, JoJo claims her championship title. I console myself with another big swig from the vodka bottle. As I tilt my head back, I accidentally smash the lip of the bottle against my mouth with a THUNK.

Shit. Shit! *Ow-ow-ow-ow!*

I yelp, "Oh my God, JoJo, I think I just broke my face!" The bottle, meanwhile, is on the rug where I dropped it, and the remaining vodka is glugging out all over the floor. JoJo is half freaking out about the rug, half hysterically laughing at me. I curl into the fetal position on the couch, clutching my mouth, while JoJo mops up the puddle of vodka with her orange hoodie.

The intense pain in my lip finally starts to fade, as does JoJo's totally unsympathetic cackling. She tips the bottle into her mouth and polishes off the last drops.

"See, Kels, *in* the mouth is the idea." She plops down onto the couch next to me. "Were you held back in kindergarten for poor hand-eye coordination, by any chance?"

"Hardy har, you are hilarious," I say, scowling at her.

JoJo blinks and her mouth actually drops open.

"What?" I demand.

She just gapes at me like I have three heads, and then starts to grin.

"What?"

She goes, "Look in the mirror, that's what." And dissolves in another fit of giggles.

I sigh, figuring if I have to get up anyway I can at least grab some snacks from the kitchen.

I stumble a bit heading into the kitchen. Once there, I grab a couple of Cokes from the fridge and a box of Oreos from the snack cabinet. Then I go to the hall mirror and look at myself. I look totally normal, if a smidge bleary eyed. No blood or anything. A little puffy redness on my upper lip, but that's it. What the eff?

I shout toward the TV room, "JoJo, what is your prob—"

The second I start talking, I see it. Half my front tooth is *gone*!

Oh my God. I look like the scary witch lady from *The Princess Bride*! All I need is some dirt on my face and a big cane made from a tree branch. This is not going to go over well with the folks back home, methinks.

I race back into the living room, shouting, "What am I gonna do? I look like a—"

JoJo is practically having a seizure, she's laughing so hard. She wheezes, "An old-timey hobo? A 'before' picture at the dentist's office? A vic— A vic-vi-victim of the beatdown?!" She can barely squeak out her last piece of creative genius, as her air intake appears to be constricted by mirth.

"JoJo! What am I going to do?! This is really, really bad—much worse than the time you dyed my hair purple. At least that washed out!"

But there's no talking to her. She's rolling around on the vodka-soaked carpet, snorting "victim of the beat-down," whatever that means. I may have to smother her with a couch cushion. No court in the world would convict me.

I decide that, since I do not have direct access to dental insurance, the only thing to do is call home and explain. It's only midnight, after all. Maybe my mother will not be her usual oppressive self and will instead intuit that I am at a time in my life where things are changing, and that I need the freedom to experiment with alcohol and boys without worrying about silly things like consequences and repercussions. Yes! She will realize that her best course of action will be to offer unconditional love and understanding. Perhaps she will even reflect upon the memory of a similar time in her own life (about eight thousand years ago) when she and my dad probably sat around dropping acid and twirling their love beads and wearing John Lennon sunglasses or whatever.

It could totally happen.

I call my house. My mom picks up, sounding sleepy, and

mumbles, "What's wrong?" (Why does she *always* answer the phone that way? So annoying.)

Deep breath. Must try to sound completely sober. "Mom, don't freak out. I froke—I *broke* my front tooth—it's, um, sort of totally chipped in half."

I can practically see her snapping to attention and sitting up in bed. She now sounds completely awake, and hollers, "*What?* How the hell did you do that?"

Moment of truth.

"Well, JoJo's mom got these awesome old-fashioned root beers for us, you know, the kind in the glass bottles? And JoJo was telling me a really good joke, and I guess I laughed too hard because, um, I hit the bottle right into my tooth. And it just chipped off!"

Shockingly, and despite JoJo's dancing on the couch and making faces at me, Mom totally buys my lame excuse and even agrees that coming to pick me up right now would be unnecessary. And really, lying in this specific instance is the right thing to do—I mean, there's no need to worry her. After all, she'd just have a conniption and ground me for the rest of my life, which would stunt my growth as a person. Plus I'd probably develop an allergy to Nancy the Cat from being home all the time, which would mean Travis would have to give her up and then *her* growth would be stunted by depression and the whole domestic unit would fall to pieces. So as much as I hate lying, I'm doing it for the good of my family. I am so proud of myself for being unselfish that after I hang up, I treat myself to a thousand Oreos. Yum.

I can only enjoy them on one side of my mouth. But still.

The next morning, I feel like someone poured cement over my entire head and let it dry overnight. My mouth tastes like an old sock—a chocolate sock, but still not good.

I crawl to the bathroom after spending about a week locating my glasses, which were miraculously unbroken and underneath the pajamas that I should have put on but apparently just threw on the floor before passing out. I look in the mirror, hoping that maybe my tooth won't be quite as bad as I thought, like if it magically regenerated somehow.

It is, in fact, still a disaster. I can't stop running my tongue over it, the way I did when I first got my braces off last year. It feels all scratchy and jagged.

God, my head hurts.

I shower in an attempt to revive myself, which doesn't really work, but at least I smell better. JoJo, who seems to be totally immune to the after-effects of alcohol, skips around the kitchen while I try to choke down a few saltines. She will not stop calling me a victim of the beatdown (where does she get this stuff?), so I decide I'd better slink on home.

"I'm out of here, crazy lady," I grumble. "And PS, when something like this happens to you, I hope you won't be looking to me for any sympathy. Because I'll—I'll be—"

But she isn't listening. She's laughing too hard. Hmph.

I take the subway home, lurch into my house, and find my mother in the kitchen doing her crossword (surprise). I try to sneak past her up to my room, but she is too fast for me in my injured state.

"You look horrible!" she exclaims. "Did you get any sleep at *all* last night?"

"Gee, thanks, Mom. I dunno—I think maybe I'm coming down with something. I'm just going to go to bed and—"

"We're supposed to be going shopping for something to wear to Cousin Lainie's bat mitzvah, Kels. You have nothing to wear that doesn't make you look like the ragpicker's child."

"Mooooooom! I can't go out in public with half a tooth! And anyway, that bat mitzvah isn't till May!"

"Oh, right, your tooth. I guess I'll have to call Dr. York's office."

"So . . . do you think he can see me on Monday? I'm totally down with missing school."

"Yeah, I'll bet you're down with that. Not happening. Don't you have a history test?"

Argh. My mother is unstoppable in her madness. "Mom, I can*not* go to school like this. Do you really expect me to be able to focus on a test when my face has been dis*figured*?"

She looks up at me, smirking. "Lemme see."

I show her. She barely stifles a laugh. "An old-fashioned root beer bottle, huh?" she says in this sly, annoying way. "You don't say. I'll have to ask JoJo's mom where she got those." Then she goes back to her puzzle. Without looking up, she adds, "Don't you have some studying to do?"

Note to self: Mother may not actually be fooled by brilliant white lie. Looks like I'll be going to school with half a tooth. If I have learned nothing else from living in this cesspool of insanity, it's when not to press my luck.

23

As it turns out, no one even notices my tooth on Monday, partly because I keep my lips tightly clamped shut all morning, but mostly because someone was even drunker and more careless than I was over the weekend. The whole school is talking about this junior, Lenny Pitcher, who got a *face tattoo* in New Jersey using a fake ID. It's a giant lightning bolt down one cheek, and is seriously the most hideous thing I've ever seen. Bad for Lenny, but definitely good for me.

After second period we all have to go to the auditorium for the biannual sports awards assembly. When I heard about it at the beginning of the year, I had fantasized that maybe I'd win something for my prowess as JV soccer's star left wing, but now it's just another boring assembly to get through. At least I get to miss econ.

The gym teachers clamber up to the stage and start talking about team mentality and self-confidence and other things that are not the actual reasons people play sports in high school. Then they start giving out the awards—

MVP, Most Improved, Looks Best in a Helmet, etc. There are guys' and girls' teams to get through, and though some people (the winners) are very excited, I am bored senseless.

I lean over to whisper in Em's ear. She had planned to come to JoJo's, too, but Em's mom was being grouchy and made her stay home at the last minute. "I'm holding you responsible for what happened on Friday night, you know. If you had been there, I never would've ended up looking like a jack-o'-lantern on crack!"

"Pleeeaaassseeee," she hisses back. "No one told you to guzzle down a whole bottle of vodka! Besides, it's not *that* bad. No one has even noticed."

"You are supposed to be the sensible friend! You can't leave me alone with the crazy one—I'm not strong enough to withstand her powers of anarchy!"

Em giggles, and a teacher on the aisle gives us a death-ray glare. I sit back in my seat and whisper out of the corner of my mouth.

"See? Your positive influence on me is fading! Soon I'm going to—"

"Oh, Megan won!" Em squeals, standing up with a bunch of people in our section and clapping. Our friend Megan goes up to the stage to accept the prize for something to do with field hockey. I clap for her and simultaneously check my watch. Less than two hours till my appointment with Dr. York. As long as I keep breathing through my nose and don't talk to anyone besides Em and

JoJo, no one will ever know about my run-in with the end of a bottle. Excellent.

"I'm really psyched for her," Em is whispering to me. "She worked so hard at field hockey camp this summer; she was telling me about it during—"

". . . captain of the girls' junior varsity soccer team, Julie Nelson," Coach Cantwell is saying on stage. Julie bounces up to the podium. More applause. She presents the MVP Award for girls' JV soccer to a sophomore who's unbelievable at defense. I turn around and give Lexi a sympathetic look, but she makes a "no big deal" face.

Julie goes on for a few minutes, and I cheer loudly for my teammates. I whisper to Ana, who's on my other side, "I'm amazed Julie didn't give the awards to herself!"

"Oh, she doesn't choose, the coaches do. Otherwise, yeah, I'm sure she would!"

"So really all she does as captain is yell at us and organize someone to bring orange slices to games? That's—"

". . . extra category this season, the Unsung Hero Award. It's for someone who maybe wasn't the best athlete or scored the most, but achieved in other ways, like persevering in a difficult game situation." Julie's voice has gone totally flat, like she's reading off a script. She looks pissed. What's her deal?

"So, yeah, the winner is Kelsey Finkelstein." She zips through the sentence so fast, it takes me a moment to register that she just called my name.

"Oh my God!" Em shrieks. "Get up there, you won!" Ana pushes me out of my chair and I head to the little stairs that lead up to the stage.

I won a prize? I can't believe it! I can hear JoJo yelling for me from somewhere in the back of the room, and all my friends on the team are cheering like crazy. This is so cool— I've never won *anything* before! Well, except an Etch-A-Sketch at my cousin's birthday party when I was six. Which hardly counts, especially since I forgot it on the table when we left. I'm still pissed about that, actually.

I float up to the podium, where Julie's face looks like an angry thundercloud of doom. I grin at her; I can't help it. She hands me a piece of paper that looks like a diploma with a big gold sticker on it, then gives me the least genuine hug I've ever received, which makes me smile even bigger. *This must be killing her!*

"Just so you know, this award is total BS," she sneers into my ear. "And nice tooth, by the way."

Crap! I forgot all about the tooth!

She pulls away, giving me a super-fake smile. I keep my lips glued together as I head back to my seat. No one could've seen the tooth from all the way up on stage, I'm sure.

My mother picks me up at lunch to take me to the dentist. I can't believe I made it without a single person (Julie doesn't count, because she is inhuman) finding out about my tooth. My lips hurt from all the clamping, but it's worth it.

The second I get in the car, it starts: the same conversation we've been having every moment since I came home from JoJo's. "You know, I just loved old-fashioned root beer as a kid. We lived right near a factory that made the bottles—probably the same kind you guys had the other night—and they used to get all kinds of tourists who'd visit to see how the bottles were made—."

"Mom, I thought you grew up in Queens."

"And your grandma Gertie *loved* root beer . . . maybe we should pick up a case on the way back from the dentist. Did you know root beer was originally made from sassafras?"

At the dentist, Dr. York sort of glops some stuff on my tooth and then shines a UV light on it while I sit there in a lead bib and crazy mouth holder-opener. When it's sufficiently UVed, he starts filing away at it, which is the worst noise ever and totally freaks me out. I think, *What if I grind my teeth at night or something? Is the whole thing going to fall off again?* I'm about to ask Dr. York, but he dashes off to see another patient and my mom is tapping her watch at me in the doorway to the exam room.

I'm afraid that my days of fearlessly enjoying Laffy Taffy are over. But at least I look normal.

On the ride back to school, my mom starts in about the damned root beer again, so I cut her off by telling her about my surprise win at the sports assembly. But that only distracts her from the history of root beer for a few minutes, so in a last-ditch effort I bring up auditioning for *Fiddler on the Roof.*

BINGO. That jump-starts a *thrilling* discussion of my mother's college drama experience, which consisted of being in some play with a guy who later was on some sitcom I never heard of. Apparently, this makes *her* practically famous.

"Are you doing a monologue for your audition, Kels?" she asks. "A classical monologue? Or a modern piece—something by Edward Albee, maybe? It's so exciting that you're interested in the arts. I'm glad you're finally taking after me!"

Then she starts performing a scene from her college tour de force in an insane Southern accent. I'm just about to strangle myself with my seat belt when we pull up in front of school. I haven't been this excited to be here since the first day.

"Thanks, Mom! Great talk. Nice acting. See ya." I start getting my stuff together to make a fast break for it, but she seizes the strap of my bag.

"Hold it, Kelsey," she says. "Now you listen up—*no more stupidity.* I know you think it's okay to act out and be Typically Adolescent, drinking till you're sick and who-knows-what-all, but know this: I won't bail you out if you get arrested. Do you understand me? You'll just have to spend the night in jail. You get one pass on this kind of behavior, and you used it up on Friday. Are we clear?"

So it seems she was onto me all along. Couldn't she have just *said* that instead of torturing me with root beer trivia? I'm all, "Gee, Mom, I'll try really hard not to join a gang and murder anyone so you don't have to deal with it. Yeah, so, that's the bell—gotta go." I grab my bag and run for my life.

Mothers. Le sigh, l'exhaustion.

I'm halfway to my history class, digging through my bag for a LUNA bar, which I'm planning to try to eat with the left side of my mouth only, when I almost run smack into the snarky guy from the newspaper office.

Okay. He's exactly as cute as I remember, and probably just as aggravating. *Please, God, don't let my new tooth fall off while I'm talking to this guy.*

"Hey, it's *The Reflector*'s angriest subscriber," he says, grinning in his maddening way. "Kelsey, right?"

I scowl at him. "I'm not a subscriber, I'm a victim of circumstance. And I'm not angry, I'm—"

"Ecstatic to be part of the periodical landscape?"

"Oh, yeah, well," I reply. *Oh, good, Kelsey, that's a terrific comeback. Well, less talking is better—don't want to disturb the tooth.* "I'd rather just view the, uh, landscape from, uh—what are you talking about?"

He laughs, his dark eyes squinting almost closed. "I'm

just playing with you, chill. Hey, how's your friend? She get an assignment yet?"

"You mean Lexi?" *He remembered* my *name but not hers?* "Yeah, I think she's working on an article or something."

"Good. And, hey, congrats on the award this morning. Nice job."

"Oh. Well, thanks. It was a big surprise, let me tell you."

"You looked pretty psyched about it."

He stares at me. I stare at him. I should say something now. Um. "So, did you tell your editor about the picture thing?"

Oh, perfect. Get back to being the angry girl.

"Yeah, don't worry; I mentioned it to Kate. She felt bad about it, so it's a good thing you stopped in. I was glad you did, anyway."

You were? "Oh, were you?"

"Yeah, it can get pretty boring working during lunch hour. Not every day an outraged young lady barges in and threatens the life of a staff member, you know?"

"Oh. Well, right. So . . . thanks? I mean, you're welcome? I mean, uh—"

"Hey, dude, you coming or what?" A voice shouts from down the hall. I see a trio of older guys I don't know heading toward us.

"Nice, man—taking time out for the laaaaadies." A second guy smirks, giving me a lame once-over. "Speaking of which, Val's looking for you. As usual." The other two laugh, at what I don't know, and then all four erupt in some standard arm-punching and pseudo-wrestling. I decide to get out of the way before I lose another tooth.

I sneak a peek behind me as I walk away. Newspaper Guy is looking right at me. Dammit! Now I feel even more like a tool. He lifts his eyebrows at me mischievously, then smoothly turns and heads off with his friends.

Hot or not, that guy thinks he is way too awesome.

I definitely shouldn't have turned around.

24

Audition day for *Fiddler* arrives before I have time to blink, but since I spent two whole hours last night practicing the song from *Wicked* in front of my bathroom mirror (when not procrastinating by reenacting the run-in with the newspaper guy, only with me sounding less like a dolt), I feel pretty confident about the whole audition business. I also decided it would actually be best *not* to listen to the original version of the song or look it up on YouTube, so I wouldn't be influenced by anyone else's dramatic choices.

The school day finally grinds to a halt and I head to the drama building with Em. It seems that Cassidy auditioned at lunch because she had a voice lesson right after school, and afterward she loudly proclaimed in history class that she *definitely* will be getting a lead role in the show. Well, we'll just see about that, Ms. Freshman Theater Wannabe.

Em and I sit down in the hall outside the theater to wait for our turns; she closes her eyes and I can see her lips moving as she mentally rehearses her song. I sort of pretend to do math homework while going over my song in my head at the same time, which I think makes me look less nervous. But after seeing how nervous everyone else is, it's suddenly occurred to me that this play audition thing might be the worst idea I've ever had in my life and I should definitely head home immediately. *What was I thinking?* Maybe I'll go over to the *Reflector* office and offer to organize their photo database. Or start a Save the Manatees Club. Anything, really, but stand up alone on a stage and sing in front of people.

Mr. Zinner comes out and calls Em's name. I squeeze her hand and she goes into the theater. Now it's just me and a bunch of people I don't know. Waiting. I'm just about to start hyperventilating when JoJo comes dashing down the hallway.

"JoJo, what are you doing here?" I slide over so she can sit down next to me.

"I decided to audition after all. Why not?"

"What? I just saw you last period and you didn't say anything! When did you decide, like five minutes ago?"

"Yeah," she says, grinning. JoJo Andover strikes again. "What did you decide to sing?"

"This song called 'Defying Gravity,'" I tell her. "It's from—"

"From *Wicked*?"

"Yes! Why, have you seen it?"

"Yeah, my mom knows the makeup designer or someone and we got house seats. But Kels, did you listen to the album or anything? That's a *really* hard song."

I sigh. "JoJo, I played it about a million times on the piano. It's not really that hard."

She looks at me like, *Okay, it's your funeral.*

"Maybe I'm just very musical. Has that ever occurred to you?"

"Well, at least your tooth looks normal again. So that's good, right?" I thwack her on the arm. "Sorry! You'll be great. I have total faith in your amazing musicality!"

Em comes out and Mr. Zinner calls for JoJo to go in. "How was it?" I ask Em.

"Not so bad, actually. You know, you just stand on the stage and sing and they say thanks and that's it. No big deal, really."

But a few minutes later, JoJo comes out, shaky, pale, and looking like she's about to vomit. And before I have a chance to ask how it went, I am summoned.

I walk to the piano and hand over my music, then climb up onstage. I try to pretend that this is actually a reality show that I'm watching instead of the most terrifying moment of my life. It helps a tiny bit.

Mr. Mackler, the music teacher, kind of gives me a funny look when he sees my song selection, which is annoying, but whatever. Does no one have faith in me? Geez.

He starts to play the introduction. I have to say, the song

sounds a lot more complicated with all those extra notes in there. I feel this huge gush of nerves in my stomach, and I realize I'm not entirely sure where to look while I'm singing. At Mr. Zinner's combover? At the empty chairs out in the audience? Do I pretend I'm talking to someone on the stage?

Then it's my cue . . . I come in for my first note, but for some reason the guy's playing it, like, an entire octave up from where it belongs. I stick to the way I'd practiced it—nice and low. I keep going, throwing in some arm movements for good measure (and distraction?), but I'm thinking, *Is it possible I practiced this an octave below where it should be? No. That's ridiculous. Right?* I soldier on. Hmmm. The end sounds like it should be much bigger than I thought with Mr. Mackler playing the piano all high and swirly like that with big chords and arpeggios and things. *Ugh, just let me out of here already!*

Finally, it's over; Mr. Zinner and the others sort of look at one another and then at me. Are they smiling? Is that an at-me or a with-me smile? Not sure. I quickly mumble thanks and bust out of there. And just like that, my first theatrical audition is over.

Em is waiting outside. "How'd it go?"

I grimace. "Not sure. I think I might have stunk, actually."

"Oh, come on—I'm sure you were awesome! You think we might both get cast?"

"I dunno," I reply. "I guess we'll find out soon enough, though. Hey, where'd JoJo go?"

"Bathroom. She thought she was going to puke and didn't want an audience."

"Em, I seriously don't think I've ever seen JoJo nervous before!" I shove the *Wicked* score into my backpack.

"I know. So, should we check on her?"

"Well, I *have* seen JoJo mad. So, no—definitely not. Better to call her later."

Em laughs, linking her arm through mine, and we head for the subway station.

When I get home, I go onto YouTube immediately. There are about a thousand entries for this song, with a whole bunch of different actresses singing it. I click on one.

Gulp. Um, JoJo was right—the song is impossibly high and *hard*. No wonder Mr. Mackler looked at me funny! I sang the whole song an octave down from where it belongs—and maybe *two* octaves below at the end. Why didn't he stop me? I am mortified. *Mortified!*

This revenge plan may not turn out as well as I had hoped.

25

A week goes by. Nothing. Evidently we are going to be kept in suspense about the cast list for approximately forever.

Every time I walk past the bulletin board between classes, I see Ned Garman frantically checking it. He and his drama groupies go racing up to the board like the Holy Grail is going to be thumbtacked there if they just keep looking every five seconds. I'm tempted to stick up a random piece of paper just to watch them hustle over to read it.

But I have to admit—I'm curious, too.

On Friday, as we walk to second period together, Em and I brainstorm about what to do this weekend to take our minds off the cast list anxiety. We're almost to our classroom when Cassidy comes dashing past us in tears, followed closely by Jordan Rothman. Everyone in the hall turns and stares at them, of course, and then the whispering starts. Not like there isn't some kind of scene every day around this place, but it's different when it's someone you know.

Em and I look at each other—we know the cast list

hasn't gone up yet, so there's only one other possibility. "You think he came clean about Lori?" she asks.

"Are you kidding? I bet she caught him red-handed! Or . . . lipped. Or whatever."

"Poor Cass." Em looks like she's going to cry, too.

"Oh, sweetie. Are you . . . thinking about, you know, James?"

Well, that was definitely not the right thing to say. Em's eyes fill up with tears.

"No. I mean . . . well, a little." She sniffs, pulling herself together. "I just feel so bad for Cass. She's so crazy about Jordan. We should probably go see if she's okay, don't you think?"

"You go. She'll just think I'm there to say 'I told you so,' and anyway . . . she hasn't exactly earned my sympathy the last couple of months."

"Yeah, I know. But maybe now you guys can patch—"

"One thing at a time, Ms. Peacemaker. Go forth and bring cheer to the wounded. But do feel free to mention that I *did* actually tell her so . . . you know, if it comes up."

Em gives me a disapproving look and heads after Cassidy.

The hours drag by . . . Econ, pointless . . . Math class, boring . . . lunch, disgusting . . . English, endless . . . and *then*! At the very end of the day, there's something on the bulletin board!

The entire free world crowds around the new and official-looking piece of paper attached by assorted thumbtacks. *Even if I don't get cast,* I think, *I will be happy for Em and JoJo if they do. I will be supportive. Or at least I will fake it to the best of my ability.*

Em wriggles up to the front and gets a peek. She gives me a thumbs-up over her head. Seriously, again with the thumbs-up?! What does that even *mean*?

I spy Ned Garman leaning against a locker across the hall and feigning nonchalance, but he is definitely not *that* good an actor, because he looks over at the board every three seconds and is practically hyperventilating. Julie is with him; she seems to have forgotten about me lately and I don't want to remind her that I exist. I duck behind a tall kid with a puffy coat to stay out of her line of vision.

Two sophomore drama girls break away from the crowd and come screeching over to Ned and Julie. Apparently his brilliance is unwavering: Ned's been cast in the starring role of Tevye the Milkman.

I see Cassidy, who seems to have recovered from the Jordan-related events of this morning, push up to the front. She takes a good, long look at the list and storms away from the board, looking pissed off. This is clearly not her day. *Sweet.* Um, I mean, *Oh. That's too bad.*

Finally, I can't take the suspense for another second. I push my way up to the board and look at the bottom of the list first, where the chorus members are listed—there's Em and Cassidy. My name isn't there. I feel a tug of despair in the pit of my stomach, but I try to ignore it.

Then I look up at the main list. JoJo is the fourth name on there, as Hodel. That's the daughter with her own song—a major part. Wow! And . . . Oh my God. My name is on there, too, and it's near the *top*!

I actually got a part!

Okay, okay . . . so, who am I? I look on the character name side . . . in the row with *Kelsey Finkelstein*, it says *Lazar Wolf*.

What the heck is a Lazar Wolf? Am I playing a wolf? Is that a Native American name? I don't remember any Native Americans in the movie version of this show at all.

I'm about to call JoJo to congratulate her—and ask her if she has any clue what my part is—when Julie Nelson, with Ned in tow, looms up in front of me like the terrifying gorgon that she is.

"Oooh, Kelsey," she croons. "Looks like you have a play now, too, not just a soccer team. Isn't that great, Nedward? You can be in Kelsey's play!"

Thank you, Julie. Thanks so much.

I smile weakly at Julie and say congrats to Ned (who is still trying to look world-weary but obviously can't wait to go squealing through the streets with the news of his greatness), then I look at my phone and pretend to be composing a very important text message in the hopes that Julie will go away.

She doesn't go away. Instead she sneers, "Seriously, two freshmen with lead parts this year . . . what was Zinner

thinking? Well, I'm sure you're *super* excited about yours."
Then she looks at Ned and they both snort with laughter in
a very obnoxious way.

"Yeah, thanks, that's really nice of you. Um . . . I don't
actually know who—"

"You don't? Oh, no wonder you don't seem excited yet!"
Julie practically shrieks. "Well, Ned, why don't you tell
Kelsey about her role—after all, you two have a big scene
together, right?"

"Yes, a pivotal one," Ned says pompously. "My character's dramatic arc in Act One centers in part around—"
He shuts up when he sees Julie glaring at him. He clears
his throat. "Lazar Wolf is the butcher who asks for Tevye's
eldest daughter's hand."

Julie starts cracking up. So do several drama groupies
who have stepped away from the cast list to eavesdrop on
Almighty Ned.

I'm still lost.

"I didn't know there were women butchers in . . . um,
olden times. Was that in the movie?" I inquire.

"No, it's much better than that," Julie chokes out. "They
must've run out of guys, or maybe they just saw something
really special in you, because Lazar Wolf is"—she gasps for
air—"the fat old butcher. A *male* butcher. A big, fat, old
man. And you're playing him. Hahahahaha!"

Hahahahaha!

Wait. *What?*

26

Julie is still crying with laughter as she drags Ned off. The groupies follow them, bowing and scraping. Meanwhile, I am rooted to the spot, aghast at the news.

How could this have happened? I can't play a man! Certainly not an old fat butcher! Is this because I sang so low at the audition? Did they think I was actually a guy?

There is no way I am being in this play. *No. Way.* I mean, why?! Is God punishing me because I made three mistakes during my bat mitzvah service two years ago? Surely I can tell Mr. Zinner that I made a huge error auditioning in the first place and that I want out, right?

I storm out of school without waiting for any of my friends. By the time I get home, I'm still not sure if I should write a heartfelt resignation letter to Mr. Zinner or suck it up and try to get excited about the fact that I did sort of get a lead part. I hang up my bag and am about to holler up the stairs to see if anyone is around when the front door opens and my sister and my mom come in. Travis is munching away on a humungous ice cream cone.

"Mom, what are you doing home from work so early?" I ask suspiciously.

She bursts into tears and I think, *Oh my God, what's wrong with her? Is she sick? Does Travis have a tumor or something?* I grasp the edge of the counter and whisper, "Mom, what's going on?"

She takes a deep breath and looks down at my sister and says through the remaining tears, "Well, Travis. Tell your sister the news!"

"I'm playing Annie in the fourth-grade play," Travis announces haughtily. "That's the star, FYI."

"Wait, what? I thought someone was dying!"

"Travis is playing Annie!" Mom exclaims. "Isn't that so exciting? I always said you girls take after me, even if you look just like your father. He ruined both of you with that nose . . . Oh, Kelsey, did you have *your* audition yet? How did that go?"

I seriously cannot believe this is happening.

Would now be the best time to tell them that I, too, am about to be a big star? Yeah . . . I think not. I half listen to my mother gush over her favorite child while imagining what my life is going to be like as the next Willow Smith's pathetic, butcher-portraying older sister.

I call Em as soon as I can escape and tell her about the afternoon's events. She gets all excited about the Travis part for some reason. I mean, I guess it's very nice that Trav is going to star in *her* school play, but I kind of want Em to be more "That sucks that you got cast as an elderly, obese male butcher" and less "Travis is going to be Annie? That's so cute!"

Sometimes I think Em's only real flaw is that she's an only child.

The more I think about it, the more ridiculous this whole thing is. But why should I resign? I got a lead part—exactly what I wanted! Sure, it wasn't exactly the role I would've *chosen* . . . but so what? I said I was going to make my mark this year, and this is what I've got to work with.

No one ever said it would be *easy*.

27

Rehearsals for *Fiddler* start the next Monday afternoon, with something called a "table read." I sort of thought it would be fancier than just sitting around a table and reading, but apparently not. During the entire thing this junior guy in the chorus (who apparently coveted my supporting role and has to be the Innkeeper/Russian Soldier/Bottle Dancer instead, har har) keeps shooting me the dirtiest looks ever. Which makes me feel elated and terrified at the same time. I also learn that in rehearsals we all just wear our regular clothes and stuff, so I'm even more cheered up—I mean, is it really any more ridiculous to believe that I'm a butcher than it is for Em to be portraying a forty-year-old mother of six living in a shtetl?

It only takes a week to discover that rehearsals, contrary to what I had envisioned, are incredibly tedious and boring. Cassidy always talked about theater like it was this exclusive, fabulous thing where everyone is very serious and intense and creative—I imagined a lot of crying, yelling, waving scripts around, and having big dramatic breakthroughs. Then afterward everyone would hug each other for support or something like in *Glee*.

It turns out that instead it's mostly just a bunch of sitting around. Well, the upperclassmen definitely hug about a thousand times a day as though they may never see each other again, which is pretty weird. Also, Ned *does* wave his script around while muttering his lines incessantly. I'm surprised Julie isn't there, too, just so she can hold his script for him when he isn't waving it.

I mostly sit in the audience with Em and the other freshmen in the chorus, doing homework or eating and gossiping about school stuff. There *was* one interesting moment on the third day, though, when Ned went up to JoJo and announced, "I think it would be really beneficial to your process if we spent some time improvising as father and daughter. I'm a Method actor, like Brando. Have you seen *On the Waterfront*?"

JoJo started cracking up. Ned got really pissed and stormed backstage; now he won't talk to any of the freshmen at all. Of course, he never talked to most of us in the first place—he only deigned to acknowledge JoJo because she's a lead.

Sometimes the whole cast spends the afternoon watching Mr. Zinner and his assistant stomp around on the stage pretending to be us and whispering to each other, "Would a circle be more authentic here? Should they hold hands? Let's try holding hands and moving in a grapevine step."

At first that's pretty hilarious as far as entertainment goes, but it gets old after about two days. Especially since, when the cast *does* get to go onstage, we just stand in our places forever while Zinner and Co. run around in the audience seeing how we look from different angles.

Meanwhile, Mr. Mackler has yet to come to a rehearsal and teach us any music. On the first day Mr. Zinner announced, "Speaking the lyrics *before* singing them will help us really *understand* them. *Be* the *words*. *Feel* your *roots* in the *words*."

I don't know about anyone else, but I think since this is a *musical* we might want to learn some of the *songs*.

In the middle of the third week, Jill, the junior playing Tevye's wife, Golde, flops down in the seat next to me. "Hey, Kelsey," she says. "Want some Swedish Fish?"

"Sure, thanks!" It's pretty awesome for a junior to actually be friendly to me. I like Jill a lot; she's had a lead in the play—as a female, mind you—since she was a freshman, and I get the feeling the kids who were upperclassmen then gave her a hard time about it. Despite all the rumors about her being stuck-up and a show-off, she's super sweet.

Cassidy worships her, of course. Jill has an *amazing* voice and wants to study theater in college. She also tells us lots of good insider gossip about the drama department—like that

Mr. Zinner is having a torrid affair with Mr. Mackler and everyone knows about it, even though Mr. Zinner is always talking about all the women he supposedly "Knocks senseless with recitations of Shakespearean sonnets—something you boys might want to try" (insert creepy wiggly eyebrows here). Gross.

I swallow the Swedish Fish, then ask, "Want me to run your lines with you?"

"Ugh, I can't even look at them anymore. Who cares about whether my daughter marries a tailor or not? I'm sorry, but I hate this show. I know it's a classic, but . . . it's so boring!"

"Yeah, I said the same thing when they announced it. Why did they pick it in the first place?"

"Oh, as a showcase for Ned. They always do that for whoever the favorite senior who does drama is. He told Zinner he thought playing Tevye would look really good on his résumé," Jill explains.

"Yeah, I'm sure playing a forty-five-year-old milkman in a *high school* show is really going to impress the bigwigs on Broadway." Jill covers her mouth, laughing. I continue, "But then, Ned is seriously so deluded that he probably thinks it will."

"True. So, I got the inside scoop that we're going to actually be allowed to *move* onstage today."

"Seriously? Does Zinner really think we're ready for such an enormous challenge?"

"Apparently. We're doing the opening number, so get psyched."

Lo and behold, Jill is right—the whole cast is finally summoned to do some alleged choreography. Despite Mr. Zinner's helpfully pounding out the rhythm to the opening number on the side of the stage, we're a mess. I'm just speculating here, but it's probably because we're speaking the words to a song that's written in four overlapping parts.

"NO, NO, NO, NO!" Mr. Zinner screams encouragingly. "Actors, listen to me! You are Jewish peasants, not elephants! You have pride, you have tradition, you have love for your people! Stop that clomping! Women, let me see the love for your children! Hold them to your bosoms! Men, show me your faith in your God! Tradition! Tradition! *Traditiiiiioooooonnnnnn!*"

At least three people crack up at the word *bosoms* before Mr. Zinner has a fit and cancels the rest of the day's rehearsal.

I may have been one of those people.

The rest of the week, Mr. Zinner calms down enough to block the other big numbers. (*Blocking*, I am informed, is the theater word for telling people where to stand onstage, when to enter, move around, etc.) We're still pretty terrible, but Zinner deems us worthy of moving on anyway. That means the in-between scenes have to be dealt with.

I'm only in about three of them, so I still have to do a lot of sitting around, which bites.

I turn to Em and JoJo and ask, "Why do we have to be here at all? Couldn't we just come in on the days we're doing something?"

Before either one can answer, Cassidy says loudly, "I wish all the actors in this play knew how to be supportive of the cast as a whole and not just worry about their individual scenes. I guess we can't *all* be professionals."

Interesting, I think. *By the way, we* aren't *professionals.*

I roll my eyes at Em, who gives me a look that I know means, *Why don't you and Cass talk this out and make up so we can all go back to the way things were before?*

Fat chance. I love Em, but forget it. I know she wants all of us to be able to hang out again—instead of alternating between the three of *them* and the three of *us*—but Cass is the one who keeps making things worse. At this point, she doesn't even seem like someone I'd *want* to be friends with.

Now it's day one of week four rehearsals, and I'm in the front row of the audience doing an outline for biology class while intermittently looking over my lines, which I haven't said out loud since the table read. JoJo is in the number that's getting rehearsed onstage—something to do with brooms and an old matchmaker. I can barely tear my eyes away from the action, let me tell you.

I hear the doors at the back of the theater open and turn

to look. Oh, God. It's the cute guy from the newspaper office. Why is he here?

I try to hide behind my script as I watch the most interesting thing that's happened all week. He goes over and says something to Mr. Zinner, who nods feverishly in response. Then the guy collects Ned and Jill and a few other people with big parts in the show and they head out of the auditorium.

Huh. I guess he's interviewing them for the paper or something. I wonder what the headline will be? Maybe: "Spring Musical Guaranteed to Be Total Artistic Failure!" or "Student Actors Die of Ennui Before Show Even Opens!"

I turn back to the stage, where Mr. Zinner is now making JoJo and the other girls who play the daughters watch as he acts out all their parts himself. This includes dancing around on tiptoe, lovingly cradling a broom and then pretending to be a scary witch of some sort. He's actually not half bad. I'm starting to think it would make a lot more sense if we scrapped *Fiddler* altogether and just helped Mr. Zinner put on a one-man show.

I'm halfway through texting this idea to JoJo when there's a tap on my shoulder. I turn around. It's the paper guy. He's grinning—what a surprise.

"Hey, I thought that was you," he says, leaning against the back of my seat. "Are you actually in this play, or just filing a complaint about it?"

"Ha, ha. Very funny," I reply. "What are you doing here? Taking embarrassing pictures and ruining innocent lives?"

"Exactly! That's what we pride ourselves on doing at *The Reflector*, you know."

"Oh, believe me, I know. Hey, there's good news, though; the caf staff said I'm welcome to pick up a few extra bucks working the lunch line anytime."

See? I can laugh at myself. And hey—full sentences today! *Go me!*

Paper Guy chuckles. "Nice. Hey, Lexi wrote a great article for the new issue, by the way." *Aha! I knew he remembered her name. Now he'll probably ask me for her number, right?*

"Oh, yeah—she was really excited about it. She won't let me read it until it's published, though, so I haven't seen it yet. I'm psyched for her."

"Well, I shouldn't do this, *buuuut*," he murmurs quietly, looking around like he's about to do something extremely dangerous and top secret. It's very cute and silly, and makes me *almost* not hate him for being so cocky all the time.

He reaches into his bag, whispering now. "If you want a sneak peek at it, I *happen* to have a copy of the new edition with me. Can you keep it under your hat?"

He holds out this month's *Reflector* and then snatches it back when I reach for it. "I need you to swear! I'm breaking all kinds of protocol here!"

"Gee, I don't know," I hesitate, playing along. "I mean,

are you sure you can trust me with something of this magnitude? I've been known to cause trouble for your staff."

"Well, there's something in it I think you'll want to see, too," he says, smiling again and handing over the paper. "You'll have to let me know what you think." Really? Well, that's mysterious. I wonder what—

His phone buzzes and he glances down at it to read the text. "Oh, gotta split. See ya!"

And then he's gone. I'm about to dive into the paper to figure out what he was talking about when I'm summoned to the stage. Dammit! I shove the paper in my backpack to look at later.

We're halfway through the run-through of the opening number when I realize . . . I still don't know Newspaper Guy's name.

28

A couple of excruciatingly long hours later, I walk through my front door, thoroughly exhausted by musical theater, a certain smart-alecky boy who works on the paper, and life in general.

In a rare turn of events, my sister is actually setting the table. Of course, she is wearing the Annie costume my mother bought her, as she has been for weeks now. You know, the red dress with the little belt? She changes into it the second she gets home from school every day. I'm frankly amazed that my parents put their collective feet down about her wearing it *to* school every day. When I told my parents about the play *I'm* in, did they offer to buy me my own deli-meat slicer? No. Of course not.

All I can think about is running up to my room to look through *The Reflector*—what could possibly be in it? The train was too crowded to get it out on the way home, and it's practically burning a hole in my backpack. But I'm only halfway up the stairs when my mother hollers, "Kelsey Finkelstein! Get down here and help your sister!"

"Help her how exactly? By handing her forks?" I say, still poised with one foot on the stair above the other.

"Kelsey, please don't argue with me. I'm tired and I'm hungry and I've had it with your Typical Adolescent Beha—"

"Ugh, *fine*!" I stomp back down, hurling my backpack on the floor next to the stairs. I plan to eat as quickly as possible and make my escape.

Once we sit down at the table, Mom announces, "Girls, I need you to find out about tickets for your plays ASAP."

Travis looks up from the spaghetti she is smearing on herself and says, "Mommy, there are no tickets. It's just during assembly period one day."

"Oh," Mom says, looking miffed. I guess she won't be allowed to bring in the local news team to assembly period. Bummer. "Well, then you, Kelsey. Find out. Everyone's coming to your big debut and I want good seats."

Wait a second, what? "Uh, who is 'everyone,' exactly?"

"Well, us, of course," Mom explains. "And Daddy's partners, their wives and kids. The Goldsteins and the Eakeleys will come. We have to invite the Wurgafts and the Udells from temple—oh, and the Harrises. I'm sure Aunt Eve will want to come. Maybe some of the women from my tennis game . . . Marv, do you think your cousin Dana would enjoy the show? You know she never gets to the theater anymore . . ."

Great. Having a bunch of my parents' friends see me

portraying the thrilling role of Lazar Wolf the Butcher in a musical where everyone speaks the lyrics should be just the right mix of humiliation and trauma to help me solidify the memory forever. I won't even need a cast picture.

". . . and of course we'll include Jed!" my mother finishes with a grand flourish.

"Jed?" I ask. "Who the heck is Jed?"

"Duuuuh," Travis says, her mouth full of broccoli. "Jed is my agent."

"Agent?"

"Yes." My mother beams. "Travis is going to start trying out for commercials!"

"What? Since when?"

"Well, Kelsey, if you would stop locking yourself in your room and talking to your friends on the computer all night—what you could possibly have to say to them after seeing them all day, I can't even fathom—you would know what's going on around here!" My mother mouths "Typical Adolescent Behavior" at my dad. (Apparently Typical Adolescents don't notice things like that, even when they are occurring six inches away.) Mom turns back to me. "Travis went with her friend Jessica to a commercial audition last week and just *loved* it, so we got her all set up with Jed. And he is no small potatoes according to Elaine Rabinowitz, who would know."

Oh, of course. Elaine Rabinowitz. Whoever that is.

"So, why shouldn't Jed come see your show?" Mom

continues. "He'll love it! Two talents in one family? He'll fall all over himself!"

Uh, hello? Has everyone here lost their minds completely? I can't have some Hollywood agent at my school play—especially when there is *no chance* he will do any falling all over himself. Maybe crying. But no falling, for sure.

"Um, I think this is approximately the worst idea in history, Mom," I tell her as patiently as possible. "For one thing, the play kind of sucks. And for another—"

"Come on, Kels, don't be a downer! We're all excited about the big show." My dad looks up from the brief he's dripping sauce on to participate. "Hey, maybe you girls can do a TV show together! That'd pay for college, huh?"

"And don't say 'sucks,' honey—it's common," Mom adds pointedly.

"Guys, you know I'm playing a butcher, right?"

Mom sighs with exasperation. "Oh, Kelsey, you're exaggerating. End of story, everyone is coming, and you'll be terrific."

I don't know how you "exaggerate" being a butcher, but I guess I should be grateful for a taste of familial support, finally. And yet, only thoughts of future embarrassment come to mind.

"Mom—"

"What, Kels? Do you want to try out for commercials, too?"

Travis snorts milk through her nose. Very nice.

"Yeah, no, thanks. Okay, well, I have a lot of homework to do, so . . . yeah. Can I be excused?"

I clear my plate and dash to my room, where I discover that Nancy the Cat has puked up a hairball in the middle of my bed. Dear God, how I wish I had my own apartment. I swiftly ball all my covers together and throw them on the floor in Travis's room. Her cat, her hairball, I say. Blech.

I get out my books to finish the homework I didn't get through during today's riveting rehearsal. The newspaper with Lexi's story is tucked inside my math notebook, and I put that on top of the pile—I should definitely digest before diving into homework. I also want to call Lexi and tell her how psyched I am that her article is in the new edition.

I dial Lexi on my cell, flicking through the newspaper while the phone rings. What was that guy talking about? There's an article about the school's carbon footprint. Maybe he thinks I look like an avid recycler?

"Hey, Lex," I say when she picks up. "I just wanted to tell you . . . that I saw your article in the new *Reflector*! I'm so proud of you!"

"Thanks!" she exclaims. "Wait—how'd you get it? The paper doesn't come out until the end of the week."

"Yeah, I know. Remember that guy, the one we met that day in the office?"

"Um, *yeah*, of course! The flirty one."

"He is not flirty, Lex. He is smarmy. There's a difference."

"Ben is his name, I think," she goes on, ignoring me.

"I haven't seen him since that day, actually, but I asked around for you. He's a junior . . . ," she trails off teasingly.

"Well, that's nice," I say, not taking the bait. "Anyway, he was randomly at play rehearsal today and he gave me a copy."

"Well, see? That's flirty! I bet he likes you."

"Yeah, yeah, he's totally obsessed with me. First of all, I think he has a girlfriend named Val something—"

"What? How do you know that?"

"And secondly, he thinks I am a crazy person who smashes her own limbs on desks and yells a lot."

"Well, that part is true. But maybe he's into that." She giggles. "Now, how did you find out about the girlfr—"

"And anyway," I cut her off, not wanting to talk about Ben's girlfriend, since that has *nothing* to do with me, "he said there's something else in here that I would want to see, but I think he was just—" I flip to the back of the paper, which is the last page of the sports section.

Oh my God.

"Kels?" Lexi says after a few seconds of silence. "Hello? Are you still there?"

"Lex, I have to go. I'll call you back."

I am staring, yet again, at a picture of myself in the school paper. This one is a full-on face shot, middle of the page, resplendent with a "Kelsey Finkelstein, freshman" label. No photo credit, of course.

The shot accompanies an article about the sports awards

194

assembly and a list of all the winners. You'd think they'd have used a picture of, say, the football MVP or something. But no. The picture shows me accepting my Unsung Hero Award from Julie, smiling my face off with surprise and joy. I guess it wouldn't be such a bad picture—it might even be a *good* picture—if it weren't for one tiny thing. Which is . . .

I am missing half a tooth! All that lip-clamping to make sure no one saw . . . and now every person in the entire school is going to have a picture of it!

Deep breaths. Damage control. Lexi is on the paper. Maybe she can help? I call her back.

"So, how hard would it be to change something in the paper? I mean, this new issue your article is in."

"Uh . . . I have no idea. But if it's been printed up already, I doubt they can. Why, what happened?"

"What about Kate Izzo? Couldn't she do something? I mean, she's supposed to be in charge!"

"Um . . . I don't know, I mean . . . I've only met her for, like, five seconds. What's going on? Are you okay?" Lexi sounds really worried.

"Yeah, just . . . humiliated. Again. You'll see."

I hang up with her and flop onto my coverless bed. I've been so good about not bursting into tears since the Scarves concert—even when I got cast as Lazar Wolf!—but I can feel them brewing now.

This is so silly. It's just a picture. *Woman up, Finkelstein!* But I just don't understand why that Ben guy would want to purposely make me feel like crap. Or Kate the Editor, or whoever these clowns are doing amateur photography, for that matter—I don't even know them! Or do I? What if there's someone with a grudge against me (Julie? Danny Zifner? Cassidy?) running around school with a digital camera, gleefully plotting ways to make me look idiotic? And why doesn't the paper have a photography budget anyway? We have three different gym teachers and a separate theater building, for God's sake! There's a vegetarian menu in the cafeteria and ergonomic desk chairs in the classrooms. And they can't afford a couple of cameras that only qualified people without grudges against me are allowed to use?!

This *stinks*.

The next morning, I contemplate storming the *Reflector* office again, but decide against it. After all, it didn't do much good the last time. Maybe I only exacerbated the situation and should try a new tactic, like wearing a bag over my head at all times to avoid future photographic appearances.

Em and JoJo meet me at my locker and I show them the picture. Em shakes her head sympathetically, and JoJo doesn't even laugh once, which I know is a struggle. She is a truly good friend, I tell you.

At least I know the storm is coming this time so I can prepare to be a laughingstock on the day the issue comes out. Who really cares about the school paper, anyway, right? Maybe there will be a surprise volcanic eruption that day and people will be too busy running for their lives to read anything at all.

It could happen.

At rehearsal, our brave director announces he's been creatively inspired and wants to add a sort of performance art element to the big dream scene where Tevye lies to Golde about how his grandmother doesn't want their eldest daughter, Tzeitel, to marry Lazar Wolf.

Although I don't really understand why we can't just stick to the script, this does mean another scene for me to be in, which means I get to do something besides sit in the audience for a change. And I don't have to learn any lines for it!

The stage is set up so Tevye and Golde are in a bed (really two chairs next to each other) on one side and I'm in another "bed" with Pearl, the girl who plays my dead wife, Fruma Sarah, on the other. The idea is that while Tevye tells his story to Golde, Fruma Sarah suddenly goes flying out of our bed and into the air, where she hovers above the *other* bed and yells at Tevye about her pearls and stuff.

I personally think that Mr. Zinner just wanted to incorporate the flying apparatus left over from a production of *Peter Pan* from, like, fifteen years ago. Poor Pearl has to gamble her life on some stage-crew kid pulling a rope attached by a wire to a weird green harness she'll wear under her Fruma Sarah costume. She is terrified. And rightly so.

All that week, we work on the dream sequence, we start blocking the wedding scene, where I actually have stuff to do as well. Now that I'm finally onstage, I'm feeling much more into being in this play. I like jotting down the stage directions in my script, and I feel pretty good about my lines, too. I am trying to infuse them with personality and flair.

Of course, I have to talk in a really deep, manly voice, so maybe I'm just infusing everything with idiocy.

Also, Mr. Mackler finally came to rehearsals and we added the singing to the lyrics at last. I feel like we look about sixty-five percent less absurd now.

Three more weeks till showtime . . . oh, and did I mention *The Reflector* came out on Friday?

By Wednesday, the fallout from the paper has mostly calmed down. For that I have to thank my friends' undying love and my personal resolve to ignore any kid who asks me if I can whistle down a taxi for him, which is about half my class. But . . . it's not as bad as it could've been, I suppose. I mean, it's not like I got a face tattoo. Or maybe I'm just getting better at dealing with personal disgrace?

Either way, I haven't seen Ben the paper guy since that day in rehearsal. I'll tell you this much: hiding from me is the smartest thing he could do.

29

After another week of rehearsing, which consists mostly of Pearl trying not to cry whenever she has to go up in the harness, Ned acting like a buffoon, JoJo sneaking a toy rat into the piano and almost giving Mr. Mackler a heart attack, and so on, Mr. Zinner announces it's time to start working with lights and costumes.

Mrs. Graves, the art teacher/costume designer, wheels a giant clothing rack of costumes onto the stage and starts handing stuff out. Now, there are some other girls playing guys in the show, too, like soldiers and men in the wedding scene and stuff, and they all get big hats and gray pants to wear—not so bad. I assume that's what I'm getting, too, but she doesn't call my name.

I'm sitting there thinking, *Am I supposed to perform naked?* when Mrs. Graves comes up to me, running a pen over her clipboard and clucking her tongue. She finally says, "Ah-*ha!* Kelsey Finkelstein . . . Well, I have a special ensemble for you, hon, but we need to do a private fitting. Please come to my office during your lunch period, okay?"

That doesn't sound good at *all*. But what choice do I have?

At lunch the next day, I quickly scarf down a sandwich and head for the art room to find Mrs. Graves.

"Um, I'm here for my fitting?"

Mrs. Graves looks up and smiles. She has coral lipstick smeared on her teeth and is wearing a beige crocheted vest, which doesn't give me any new confidence in her costume-design abilities. From the back of the room, she drags out a big, moldy-looking box that looks like it hasn't been opened since the Paleolithic Age. When she opens it, I fully expect a colony of bats to come flying out.

"Okay, hon," she says, sifting through the items inside. She hands me what appears to be a very large pillow covered with brownish sweat stains. I hold it up and see it has weird puffy sleeves attached.

"Uhhhh . . ."

"That's your fat suit, hon. Just put it right on over your undies." She goes back to digging through the vault of horrors while I stand there gaping at her back. "Go on, hon. No one's coming in, the door's locked. Chop chop!"

Oh my God. A *fat suit*? A suit of fat? Great. That's just . . . great.

I can't really see a way out of this, so I strip off my jeans and shirt and yank the thing on like a bathing suit. I check out my reflection in the door of a mirrored wall cabinet; I look like a very fat snowman with a teeny-tiny head.

I turn back around. Mrs. Graves is now coming toward me with her hands full of things that smell like a basement. "Now, hon, you won't get the final effect until you're all finished. No more peeking!" She zips up the back of the fat suit and helps me put on a shirt over it, plus a weird vest with patches, a huge knee-length coat, and a massive pair of men's pants that are way too long.

"Now, I only have men's shoes here, so why don't you go ahead and wear some plain black sneakers, okay, hon? That'll be nice and comfortable for you."

Oh, yeah. Black sneakers. That'll look terrific.

"Um, Mrs. Graves, are you sure there isn't anything, less, um . . . I mean, more . . ."

"Oh, don't worry, hon—we're not done yet!"

I take some deep breaths. I knew this day would come. What did I expect, a dress? I will just be mature and make the best of things.

Mrs. Graves rummages around in the bottom drawer of her desk until she holds up something that looks like the tail of a giant squirrel. Is it . . . ?

It is.

It's a *disgusting beard*. Does this woman think I'm going to allow her to glue that onto my *FACE*?!

She must see my look of horror, because she says, "Be reasonable, hon. You're a religious Jewish man! You need a beard. And it's not like you can grow your own, can you?" She chuckles. "We won't use the spirit gum to attach it today. I'll just scotch-tape it on you so we can see how it looks. Okay, hon?"

The true horror of being cast as Lazar Wolf the Repulsive can no longer be denied. What was I thinking, going through with this? How could I have agreed to lurch around on a stage in front of my whole school, wearing a pillow in my giant pants and a skinned rodent on my face?

After some minor additions to my lovely ensemble (a busted fedora and plastic butcher's apron. *Why?*), I'm finally shown to the mirror.

I look like Pavarotti—if he were grilling at a barbecue. In seventeenth-century Russia.

I will myself not to cry. Maybe no one will know it's me.

30

"Come oooooooon—it'll be fun. And you don't even have to wear a beard!" Lexi exclaims.

"Very funny," I grumble, thumbing through a rack of lovely shirts I will never own. I'm with Em and Lexi at Anthropologie on Saturday afternoon. "You guys go. Come find me after and let me know how it was—I'll be the one in the moldy fat suit rocking back and forth on the floor of my closet."

Lexi wants us to go to an upperclassmen party tonight that Robby, the guy she decided to go to winter formal with, invited her to. But since my big costume reveal, I'm just too grouchy to go anywhere that involves socializing. I want to sit at home and feel sorry for myself, and that is *it.* I can't believe I even got talked into coming out this afternoon . . . but I'm a sucker for this store, and Em can be very sly when she puts her mind to it.

"Kels, I'm sure your costume isn't as bad as you're making it sound," Em says. "And besides, we haven't all gone to a party together since Halloween! How sad is that? There might be cute boys there. . . ."

I look up from the bracelet I was admiring, surprised. Em hasn't talked about guys at *all* since James broke up with her. She's actually smiling at me, excited by the idea. Oh, man. Am I really going to refuse to do something that would make my very best friend happy after she's been so sad for months? I'm *used* to having everything go wrong and being miserable, so I can handle it. Watching Em be depressed is awful.

Lexi jumps in. "Oh, come on, there will be *tons* of cute boys there, and not just from our school, either. And you know who will definitely *not* be there?"

"Who?" I ask. "Me?"

"Nooooooo, and nice try," Lexi continues. "Julie Nelson! The guy who's having the party *hates* her. Apparently she hooked up with his best friend's sister's boyfriend, like, two years ago and it was a *huge* scandal."

Hold the phone: Someone who hates Julie is having a party, and I'm invited?

Just tell me when to show up. I'll bring the cake.

I spend about a thousand years getting ready, and agree to meet JoJo and Em outside the party at exactly 10:00 P.M. so we can all go in together. (Lexi's going to come with Robby.)

My cab pulls up in front of the apartment building and

I see JoJo waiting outside. I run up and she gasps, "Thank God—it is *freezing* out here! And it's the end of March, WTF?!" Her hair streaks are bright green now and she's only wearing one glove—she probably lost the other one somewhere.

We've just decided to go wait in the lobby to avoid frostbite when Em's cab pulls up.

Em gets out . . . followed by Ms. Cassidy Gayle Rosenblum.

NO. EFFING. WAY.

I don't want to make a scene in front of the doorman, who is glaring at us suspiciously already, so I grab Em's hand and we go in through the same section of the revolving door. "How could you?" I hiss at her.

"Come on, Kels! You can't stay mad forever! She's your friend! I know she wants to make up."

I pull Em to a corner of the lobby, glancing back outside, where Cass appears to be having a similar conversation with JoJo. "Em, I cannot believe you set me up to be ambushed! What did you think was going to happen? This is so awkward and horrible!"

"I don't know, I just thought . . . I hoped maybe, if you weren't expecting . . ." Em looks at the floor miserably.

Oh, Lord. I know she meant well, but this sucks. What am supposed to do? Go be the "bigger person"? I already tried that and it blew up in my face.

"Look, don't . . . don't worry about it," I tell Em. "It'll

be fine. Cass and I ignore each other at rehearsal every day and I'm sure we can do it here. This'll be great practice for the cast party. Okay?"

"Okay. I'm sorry. I just really want you guys to make up."

"I know. But next time, write a poem about it instead or something. Deal?"

Cass and JoJo come over to us. Cass and I avoid looking at each other and say nothing. Great. Can I go home now?

After getting past the scary doorman, the four of us head up to the twenty-sixth floor, where we can hear the party all the way down the hall. We go inside and there are a million people crammed into the apartment. Finding Lexi in this crowd might take all night.

JoJo and Cass go in search of drinks while Em and I take a lap around the party. Whoever the host is, his parents have a sweet apartment (and hopefully a terrific maid service for tomorrow). A big spread with all kinds of snacks is laid out in the dining room, and there are linked speakers throughout the whole place with a great playlist going. Plus a truckload of alcohol, obviously. There are a ton of kids from my school here, but mostly older ones that I only know by sight.

Em and I head into the kitchen, where we find Cass and JoJo doing Jell-O shots with some people I don't know. JoJo holds one out to me while Em grabs a bottle of water from the fridge. I crack the plastic shot glass and down the

Jell-O; when I look up, Cass is staring at me from the other side of the kitchen counter. We make eye contact for the first time in months, and I suddenly feel terribly sad. I think about how much fun we always had hanging out . . . before the tragic concert, anyway.

I'm contemplating smiling at her, just as an experiment, when a bunch more people crowd into the kitchen, including Lexi.

"Hey! You guys made it! I knew you'd cave, Kels," she says excitedly, giving me a hug. When I pull away, Cass has already turned around, chattering to some guy. I grab another shot and head into the other room with Lexi.

After an hour or so I'm pretty buzzed and sort of bored. It's a fun party, but I'm just not really in a party mood. Lexi is with Robby, who is so obviously smitten with her it's almost funny to watch him follow her around. Cassidy is still in the kitchen with Em, and JoJo seems to have disappeared. I decide to go check on the status of my eyeliner and start looking for a bathroom. I'm moseying down a random hallway when I hear a voice behind me.

"Unless you want to check out a room full of golf stuff, you're going the wrong way."

I turn around and come face-to-face with the hottest guy I've ever met in person. Ever. He's got one of those really chiseled faces, kind of like Chace Crawford. He also has sparkly blue eyes that are a lot like Jordan's. A painful stab of remembered love creeps into my thoughts, but I manage to fight it off.

"That does sound fascinating, but I probably shouldn't take in so much excitement this early in the night." I hold out my hand. "I'm Kelsey Finkelstein, by the way."

My, my! Will you look who's managing to have a coherent conversation with a hot guy? Amazing!

"Yeah, it's pretty wild. You should definitely hold off if you can." He takes my hand and doesn't really shake it, but sort of clasps it. "I'm Sam. You wanna check out the terrace?"

"Sure, definitely," I agree, and follow him through some more rooms to a big glassed-in terrace that wraps around the side of the building. There are a bunch of kids out here, just drinking beers and hanging out. It's a beautiful clear night, and the view of the Hudson River from the terrace is amazing.

Lexi and Robby are out here, too, so we pull up some chairs near them and Sam hands me a beer from a cooler full of ice. I take a swig and don't even think it's as gross as I usually do.

I catch a whiff of pot and secretly hope no one offers me any. I just know I'd cough like an idiot if I tried it, and to be honest, I'm just not interested in smoking. Regardless, I feel so pathetically excited to be a freshman in the VIP section of an upperclassmen's party. *I am awesome!*

Okay, so I'm also kinda drunk. But still: *AWESOME*!

"So, you girls play soccer, huh?" Sam asks me and Lexi, putting his arm around the back of my chair. He keeps making physical contact with me, but just barely, like brushing against my leg or my arm for one second and then pulling away. It's so distracting I can hardly keep my mind on the conversation.

"Yeah," Lexi says, leaning against Robby. "It was . . . an interesting season." She catches my eye and we both start giggling. Sam looks at Robby and shrugs, offering him another beer from the cooler at his feet.

"Do you play any sports?" I ask. It turns out Sam goes to a different school way uptown, so while I'm sort of listening to him talk about lacrosse, mostly I'm calculating how long it would take me to get from my school to his school by subway if we had plans to meet up. Just in case, of course. It never hurts to be overly prepared for a romantic adventure.

So far Robby has not said a single word. Not that I care, particularly, as every molecule in my being is focused on Sam, Sam, Sam.

Sam is definitely the hottest guy I've ever seen.

Sam has first-kiss-do-over written all over him.

Sam could—

I suddenly realize I actually have to go to the bathroom for real now—beer really goes right through you. I excuse myself, find the bathroom, and while I'm washing my hands, I have a mini fantasy that when I come out,

Sam will be waiting for me by the door. And when I walk out . . . he's actually there!

He murmurs, "I was looking for you." *Oh my God, I can feel myself blushing. Thank God it's so dark in here.* "You know tonight is my birthday, right?" Sam goes on, tugging gently on a strand of my hair.

"Ohhhh—wait, this is *your* party?"

"Yep, I'm your host. With the most. Hey, you wanna see the rest of the apartment? My parents have some cool art and stuff."

"Okay," I agree, following him out. Like I really care about art right now.

We go down yet another hallway—how big is this apartment?—and Sam stops in front of a door, which he opens and leads me through. I realize we're in his bedroom, which is completely dark except for some dim track lights. We're totally alone, which I like . . . but also feel just the *tiniest* bit nervous about. I need to chill out, so I go to take another calming sip of my beer, but Sam puts his fingers around the neck of the bottle and pulls it down from my mouth. Then he's moving in toward me and whispering, "You're so cute, Kelsey Finkelstein."

I can't believe he remembered my last name! I think, and then his lips come down on mine.

Oh my God oh my God oh my—

And it's a *really* good kiss. Not like ridiculous Keith Mayhew at all. It's soft at first, with limited tongue and some interesting lip action, then more ferocious and intense. He puts his hands in my hair and kisses my ears and my neck, and I get chills everywhere. *Everywhere.*

After a long, delicious while he whispers, "We should go back to the party, huh?"

"Yeah, definitely," I sigh, but we kiss some more instead and then he laughs and I laugh and it's . . . amazing. I feel the prettiest I have ever felt in my entire life.

He guides me over to sit on the bed, still kissing, and leans me back against the pillows. I feel so excited and romantic, and so what if I'm on a bed with a boy I've known for an hour? It's just a bed. He's just a boy. Sam slides his hand under my shirt and strokes my stomach and my rib cage, and then the side of my chest—like right along the edge of my bra. It's very tingly and I definitely like it . . . even though I'm also thinking we've been in here awhile now and it's kind of rude to ditch Em and JoJo for so long and maybe I should find them in case they're looking for me.

Then he starts grinding up against me with his hips and trying to slide his hand *inside* my bra, which I know I should be cool with because it isn't a big deal, and part of me really wants to let him . . .

But I'm sort of not cool with it. I mean, I've known him for about five seconds. And it's only my second kiss ever.

And I don't want him to think I have any intention of going further than that, for sure. I pull away a little and whisper, "Can't we just, um . . . kiss some more?"

Sam whispers, "But you're so sexy . . . and it *is* my birth-day . . ." He has his other hand on the top button of my jeans now, fiddling with it.

I sit up a little, easing him off me. "I know, and, um . . . but can't we just slow down for a sec?"

"Are you serious?"

"Uh . . . yes?"

Sam takes his hand out from under my shirt and gives me a totally disgusted look that makes me want to die. "Maaaan, I knew I should've gone for your friend instead. I bet *she's* not a prude."

Then he just gets up and leaves.

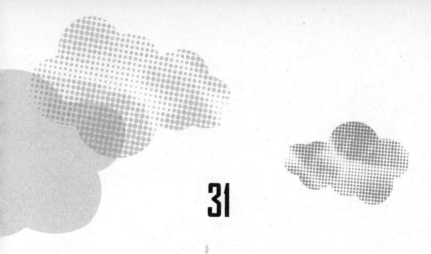

31

I fix my shirt and take a couple of deep breaths. I'm totally stunned. What the hell just happened? Am I really a prude, or is he a jerk? Does he hate me? Why do I care what he thinks? And what friend was he talking about, anyway?

My face feels raw from Sam's chin rubbing against mine, my throat is tight and constricted—tears again? *Seriously?* I just want to find my friends and get the hell out of this stupid party that I didn't even want to come to in the first place.

I really, really want to go *home*.

I'm about to open the door to leave the bedroom when it opens from the other side. A couple enters the room, whispering intently. Well, that's just *perfect*.

I try to sneak around them and out the door, but there isn't enough room, so we end up having a minor collision, which scares the girl half to death.

"Sorry! I was just leaving," I stammer, totally embarrassed. Great—now I'm a prude *and* a peeping Tom.

"Wait a sec," the guy says. "Kelsey, is that you? What are you doing in here?"

I look up from the floor, where I had been politely directing my gaze, and discover that the couple is comprised of Ben the Paper Guy and a really pretty dark-haired girl with enough self-confidence to wear glasses in public—exactly the kind of ultra-modern specs I would love to wear but can't pull off.

Why, why did it have to be him?

"I, um . . . Lexi invited me. So, I, uh . . ."

"No, I meant what are you doing in Sam's room, alone in the dark? Are you okay?" He's looking at me without a trace of his usual irony, like he's some kind of concerned big brother. Which makes me feel even worse.

No, not really. But thanks for asking. "Yeah, I'm fine. Sorry to break up your, um—"

"Ben, maybe we should go?" the girl says. She looks annoyed. I don't blame her.

He chuckles. "No, it's cool. Kelsey, this is Valentina. Val, Kelsey is blah blah newspaper blah," but I'm barely listening. It just occurred to me that Ben said "Sam's room" before, which means he knows Sam well enough to know this is his room. Which means they will probably end up talking about this whole thing later and Sam will be like,

"Oh my God, that little dork wouldn't even let me feel her up!" And Ben will think I'm a baby and a loser—more than he already does—and I will perish from an acute case of humiliation. And not because of some dumb picture in a school paper this time, but because I actually *am* a huge loser who will never have a normal hookup and will be alone forever.

"Listen, I've got to go, so, um, have fun." I push past the two of them and shove through the crowded party, desperate to find my coat and my friends and not make eye contact with anyone. Em and JoJo are both MIA, and there's no way I'm going back to the terrace to find Lexi—Sam might be out there. I just want to *leave*.

I head back into the living room, and there's Cassidy sitting on the couch with some guy. I'd rather do anything than talk to her at the moment, but I have to tell *someone* I'm leaving. So I go over to the couch and yell over the music, "I'm leaving, bye," and turn before she can say anything back. I'll just text Em and the others once I'm safely in a cab on my way home.

But Cass grabs my arm and shouts, "Wait, are you okay?"

"Like you care," I snap back over my shoulder, wrenching out of her grasp. I have to get out of here this second. I untangle my coat from the pile on the floor and book out of the apartment as fast as I can.

I'm waiting for the elevator, trying to keep the tears from

coming while I'm still where anyone can see me, when Cassidy comes running into the hall, clutching her coat and purse.

"Kelsey, what happened? You can't just run off if something—"

"Go away, Cassidy!" I pretend to be looking at my phone. *Ugh, why won't the elevator come?*

"Come on, I'm serious. What's going on?"

I spin around to face her. "Oh, so you're talking to me now?"

"Am I *talking* to you? Kelsey, I'm asking if you're okay!" The elevator doors open and I dash inside. Cassidy follows me. *Dammit. Why can't she just leave me alone with my misery?*

"Cassidy, can you please not *follow* me right now? Nothing is wrong. I just want to go home," I insist. "And you're pretty much the last person I want to be with right now, anyway." The elevator stops and some man gets in. *Awesome. An audience.*

"First of all, I don't believe you," Cassidy stage-whispers as the man looks at the ceiling. "And second, I'm trying to help you. I didn't start this fight, you know—you're the one who was, like, mad at me for hooking up with Jordan when you never even went out with him or anything! That's so unfair!"

I cannot believe the Jordan showdown is finally happening and it's in an elevator in front of a strange man on the newly upgraded worst night of my life. And since I'm still reeling from the Sam situation, I can barely even care about stupid Jordan at the moment. Also, the man is sweating. Like, a lot.

I blurt out, "Cassidy, you *knew* I liked Jordan since *forever*. We talked about it a million times! Do you have any idea how I felt when I found out you were hooking up with him behind my *back*?!"

"Kelsey, it doesn't work that way—you can't just claim a guy! And anyway, it's not like I rubbed it in your face."

"You *totally* rubbed it in my face! What do you call—"

"And then you were *sooo* happy to tell me about Lori Soler, weren't you?"

The elevator finally stops at the lobby and Cassidy stomps out. This time I follow *her*, leaving the sweaty guy behind me, shaking his head. I'm seriously pissed off, which is an excellent diversion from being devastated about the Sam thing. "I was telling you the *truth*!" I practically shout. The doorman looks over at us warily. I lower my voice but get right in her face. "I was trying to be a good friend even though you basically stole my dream guy, and you didn't even listen. You said I was pathetic and stopped speaking to me!"

The doorman has one eye on me as he says something into his walkie-talkie. I don't even care, I'm so mad.

"Cassidy, you're supposed to be one of my best friends, but you treated me like some complete stranger you couldn't care less about. You were a *total bitch* for no reason—you could've talked to me about it in the beginning instead of sneaking around. And now what? You think you're going to suddenly win a prize for friendship after months of not talking to me because you followed me out of a party when I told you to leave me *alone*? Well, sorry to disappoint you, but that's not going to happen!"

Cass opens her mouth like she's going to say something, but then she shuts it. She looks at the floor. The doorman stares at his clipboard.

Then Cass says quietly, "You're right. I *was* a bitch, and I did go behind your back. I was just, like . . . I don't know. I really liked him, too. And then I thought you were trying to get back at me with the Lori thing, and when I found out you were right about that . . . I felt like an idiot. And it was too late. But I'm really, really sorry. And I *do* want to make sure you're okay. Okay? So . . . are you okay?"

Cassidy looks all teary, and that makes the tears I've been holding back spring up to the surface. I sort of choke out, "No, I'm not okay. Can we get out of here?"

I start crying really hard as Cassidy puts her arms around me, and she leads me outside to get a cab. Through my tears, I tell her I'm so sorry I didn't find a way for us to talk sooner—I should have. She's one of my besties, after all. Then I give her the rundown on the whole Sam thing and how stupid I feel.

"This Sam guy sounds like a total d-bag, Kels," Cass says

firmly. "And don't feel dumb. You told him to get off you and he acted like a jerk. He was trying to make you do stuff you didn't want to, and that's *not* okay."

She's stroking my hair, which is very soothing, and I'm finding it much easier to breathe without choking on sobs. Which is good, because the cabdriver keeps looking at me in the rearview mirror warily, as if he thinks I'm going to puke. I stick my tongue out at him, which is incredibly immature and makes me feel a smidge better.

She continues, "Guys think they can do whatever they want. You have to be, like—"

"But didn't you have sex with Jordan?"

Oops. Well, I guess that's out there now.

Cass gasps—literally, her mouth drops wide open. "Kelsey, *no*. God, I mean, come *on*. Did you really think that? Does anyone *else* think that? I mean, we hooked up a lot. And I *thought* about it. But that is *it*. I can't believe you thought that!"

For a second, I think she's pissed at me and maybe we're back to being in a fight, but then she starts giggling like crazy. Which makes me laugh, too, even through my leftover tears.

I can't believe how relieved I am; I mean, either way it wouldn't really affect me and yet I feel so good just knowing the truth after all these months of speculating about it. So maybe there *isn't* all this behind-the-scenes heavy action going on then, at least not in my grade. Not among my friends, anyway. Which means maybe I'm not a total loser after all—well, not in terms of guys.

But I still feel completely awful about the Sam experience. I just can't help it.

32

It's been almost a week, but despite one repaired friendship and two halting but complete run-throughs of *Fiddler on the Roof*, all I can think about is what happened at the party. What I said, what Sam said, what he did, everything. Is there something about me that makes it impossible for things to work out with the guys I like? And how, I'd like to know, am I ever even going to get past first frickin' base if everyone I kiss acts like a *total jerk* five seconds later and doesn't even give me a *chance*?

I'm trying so hard not to be depressed over some stupid guy I barely know who dissed me. Em says that obviously there is absolutely nothing wrong with me, and Lexi says if she had known what was going on she would've punched Sam in the neck. JoJo and Cassidy keep insisting that it's never too late and we should go back to his building with baseball bats and crossbows.

The worst thing is, even though he's a total jerk, I still wish it had ended differently with Sam. I could be getting cute texts from him *right now,* but instead he and his friends—including Ben—are probably still laughing their heads off about it. Thank God he doesn't go to our school. Lexi swears that Robby hasn't mentioned a thing about it to her, but . . . I think she's just saying that to be nice. And no matter how hard I work to focus on other things—the show, school, my annoying family—Sam keeps sneaking back into my thoughts and I feel lousy all over again.

Friday afternoon during a free period, I'm sitting in the hall with Em, quizzing her on French verbs. She tosses her flash cards onto the floor next to her. "I hate French. I'm never going to need to speak French. I don't even like French *food*! Why do I have to learn this stuff?" she laments.

"You're asking *me*? I take Latin, for crying out loud. It's literally a dead language."

"Yeah, but that's only because your mom made you for SAT vocab prep. I *chose* French." Em takes a pack of gum out of her pocket and offers me a piece, which I delightedly accept. "So . . . Kels. Have you considered, you know, going to talk to that Ben guy again? Lexi keeps saying that he really—"

"Em, I am totally and completely done with guys. Especially any guys connected to Sam. Besides, 'that Ben guy' was supposed to make sure no more pictures of me—ugh. Never mind. Can we talk about something else? Please? Or go back to French verbs?"

"Okay, okay. But will you think about it? Because—"

"*Reluire*?" I pronounce horribly, reading off an index card.

"No, please, no! I'll stop, I swear." She blows a bubble, then quickly sucks it back in when a teacher comes around the corner.

Once the teacher is out of sight, Em asks, "So, do you think JoJo is ever going to, you know . . . say something to us? About being . . . ?"

"I don't know!" Now this is something I *would* like to discuss. "I forgot to tell you, and it was forever ago now, but the night I broke my tooth and we were wasted, I thought maybe she was about to. I don't know what to do—are we supposed to ask her about it? I don't want to rush her, and we could be totally wrong. I mean, just because she's made a couple of comments randomly—"

"Kels, it's more than that. I can't really explain it, but . . ."

"Yeah, yeah, I know." I lean back again the row of lockers. "Are we being bad friends? I want to handle this correctly! Don't we have any other gay friends we could ask?"

"Um. Matt Klausner?"

"He's gay?"

"Isn't he?"

"This is a disaster." I tap a pencil against my thigh. "What about . . ."

"You don't think she thinks we wouldn't understand, do you?" Em asks seriously. "I would feel so terrible if she did."

"I know, me too."

"So what do we do?"

"I think nothing. Right? I don't know—wasn't there anything about this in *The Secret for Teens*?"

"Nope. Although," Em adds, brightening, "there was a fascinating chapter about power relationships that would really be helpful for you to read regarding your thoughts about guys right now. If you want to borrow—"

Just then, Cassidy comes dashing down the hall and sits beside me, clutching a bathroom pass in her hand. Since we made up the night of the party, things have been so much more fun, especially in play rehearsals. "Guys!" she says excitedly. "You'll never guess what—I'm in Spanish class right now and this girl told me that Lori Soler dumped Jordan. Can you believe that?"

Em and I look at each other and then at Cass. "So?" I ask. "Don't tell me you still like him!"

Cass pouts, sticking out her lower lip like Travis does when she's not getting her way. "Well, I don't know. I mean . . ."

"Cass, you deserve someone better than him," Em interjects. "Right?"

"I guess." Cass scrambles up to her feet. "Anyway, I gotta go. See you guys at rehearsal." And she heads off down the hall.

Em peers at me, concerned. "Are you okay? I mean, is that weird for you guys to talk about Jordan now?"

I scoff. "Em, I am telling you—boys are the last thing

I'm concerned with at the moment. Besides, I'd rather have Cass than stupid Jordan any day."

"Yeah, he's terrible. Ben, on the other hand . . ."

"*Nager*!" I say loudly, reading off a card.

Em sighs. "That is totally not how you pronounce that."

33

On Monday, the day of the first dress rehearsal, I'm in the women's dressing room trying to get ready without anyone seeing me. But the second I pull out my fat suit, it starts; by the time I get my stylish black sneakers on, everyone is laughing hysterically. Of course my friends all look normal with their long skirts and kerchiefs—not to mention makeup. JoJo practically chokes to death when I put on my lovely apron and hat, which sets everyone else off all over again, too. If she weren't one of my dearest friends, I would have to strangle her with my beard.

I try to laugh it off, like, "You know, this is really helping me get into character, you guys, thanks. Oh, and by the way, I'll be sure to remember this when I'm writing my will."

I knew I should have quit this stupid play! I knew it, I knew it. I'm never not listening to myself again.

Despite everything, though . . . I'm sort of excited to see if we can pull this thing off.

. . .

The dress rehearsal actually goes smoothly—a couple of dropped cues, a minor problem with the scenery, and the one freshman guy in the cast let out a huge fart during the last number . . . but mostly it's not bad for a school play. I felt really good about my part, too.

And I can't believe how amazing JoJo is—her voice floats along during her big song like . . . well, something extremely floaty. She absolutely steals the show. I've never seen her look so innocent and sad and just sort of *into* anything before. I mean, she really becomes the character.

It's so weird that we never knew she could sing and act like that, though pretty typical of JoJo to just one day decide to be an actress. Of course, I also won't be surprised if after this she's never in a play again because she's taken up pottery instead. Or surfing. Or wild gamekeeping.

Cass is so mad watching JoJo's solo from the wings with me and Em that her lips turn white from pursing them. She's a very good sport, though. I mean, she doesn't light the stage on fire or anything. Watching Cassidy watch JoJo is the most entertaining part of the play, to be honest. It's so enthralling, in fact, that I almost forget about my costume.

Almost.

Then, in a flash, it's opening night—with my family and everyone they've ever met out in the audience, not to mention half the school. And peeking out from behind the curtains at all those people out there, I have to admit I feel really nervous. Nervous—but ready.

But first we must endure an "Energy Circle of Love," as directed by the illustrious Ned. Mr. Zinner gives a long speech about the theater gods who give us our creative spirit, then we have to do this thing I remember from Brownie camp where you "pass the pulse" around the circle by squeezing the hand of the person next to you. Ned, Jill, Cassidy—even JoJo—seem to be taking it very seriously, but I think it's extremely silly. Only focusing on my tragic patch-covered vest (and giant pants) keeps me from laughing out loud.

Being onstage, however—actually *doing* the show— is out-of-control exciting in a way I never anticipated. The lights all working finally, the audience out there in the dark clapping or coughing or laughing, the energy on the stage, everyone getting the harmonies right in the opening song—I mean, it's really happening!

When the time comes for my lines, I feel surreal saying them, like someone else is talking through me. I briefly get really scared I'll forget my next line even while I'm saying it, but I don't make a single mistake. Who knew that the dull rehearsals, the weeks of remembering which was stage right and which was stage left, the going over and over the steps for the finale would end up being worth it and actually . . . fun?

The show goes off pretty much without a hitch two nights in a row. Mr. Zinner is really proud of us. Ned is *extremely* proud of himself. My parents—and their friends—beamed all over the place and brought me a huge bouquet of roses. Travis said I looked like a real man and that my play was almost as good as hers. Also quite touching. (Thankfully, Jed the Agent stayed home, so he didn't have an opinion.)

And then, it's the last performance day—a Saturday, so we have two shows, one in the afternoon and one at night. We've just gotten through the matinee, had a dinner break, and are raring to go for the evening performance. I'm feeling a little sad—I mean, all that work and in two hours it'll all be over. I don't know how professional actors deal with it. No wonder so many of them are depressed and have substance abuse problems.

Once the curtain goes up, everything goes along as usual—in fact, the opening number gets the biggest applause yet and Motel the Tailor makes it through his song without mixing up any of the words.

Then we get to Mr. Zinner's innovative dream sequence, the one with the two beds onstage. And it's at this point that, without warning, everything falls apart.

Ned is saying his opening lines about his grandmother and I feel Pearl squeezing my arm, the signal for me to hook the wire—hidden in the bed—to her harness. The stage crew's cue comes . . . and up she goes!

The audience gasps, surprised, like they're supposed to. But Pearl does something she *isn't* supposed to: she sort of throws in a new hand gesture as she's going up into the air. It wouldn't be a big deal except the gesture catches me in the side of the head, and her bracelet gets hooked into my beard. And suddenly my dreadful, heinous beard (somewhat deteriorated anyway from being glued on and removed over and over) starts to detach from my face.

Crap! Do I grab the beard? Help, God, oh, please—this is a Jewish play, you should be doing something to save me!

I grab the beard, but too late; most of it goes up in the air dangling from Fruma Sarah's wrist, and the other sad blob of it falls off in my hand.

The audience totally loses it—and, really, who can blame them? There's a weird ghost lady hanging in midair from a totally visible wire, balling a fake beard into her sleeve, while her "husband" is suddenly exposed as a girl with a face covered in patchy glue bits. They laugh so loudly I can't even hear Ned singing anymore.

I decide to improvise—I pull the bedsheet up over my face and pretend to be cowering in fear. This gives me the chance to realize that my entire face is on fire: sudden beard removal plus spirit gum equals *unbelievable pain*. I think I may have lost an entire layer of skin.

Above me, Pearl, in a last mad effort to fix the situation, throws her half of the beard in my direction as the wire pulls her across the stage. Unfortunately, beards are very lightweight generally, and it floats through the air for what seems like forever until it finally lands on the stage next to the bed. The audience roars.

At the end of the scene, I run for my life. Mrs. Graves is backstage, totally freaking out, because the section of beard I still have is all gummed up and unusable, the other half is on the stage, and the crusty glue on my face makes me look like I have a bad case of leprosy. Mrs. Graves goes rummaging around in her costume box, but the only other beard she has is a long fluffy white one.

"You can't go out with nothing, hon! Just wing it!" she cries, slapping some glue on the beard and jamming it on my chin. Before I can protest, she shoves me onstage for the wedding scene.

Now I look like an out-of-work Santa Claus who just woke up in an alley after a three-day booze binge. In an apron.

I run over to where Ned is and try to say my lines about a gift of chickens for the wedding, but the girls playing the daughters—including JoJo—are standing behind him and turning bright red trying not to laugh at my new facial accessory. One of them finally lets out a little snort of laughter, which sets off the others. Ned's face is like a thundercloud; the audience, however, is having a grand old time.

I try to salvage the situation by ad-libbing. "Shalom, Tevye," I say in an extra-deep voice. "I brought you these chickens! But I'm so upset about not being able to marry Tzeitel myself that my beard has turned white!"

Apparently, ad-libbing is even worse than losing a beard in a freak gesture accident, especially if you can't back it up. I suddenly realize that in the rush to get a new beard, I forgot to grab my big prop: a crate of fake chickens. Ned looks more furious than ever. I try again to repair the damage with, "Um, I mean, *those* chickens. The ones outside, in the, er, barn!" Then I point to stage left.

Ned starts to respond, but at that moment the worst thing of all happens. The stage crew is supposed to turn on a fan to blow red and yellow flower petals onto the stage—another terrific symbolic inspiration of Mr. Zinner's—during the song "Sunrise, Sunset." But I guess the crew got confused or something, because the fan goes on way too early. Instead of blowing petals, the gust of air blasts my discarded original beard right off the floor. It flies up and sort of hangs in midair, held up by the breeze. And . . . it happens to be hanging in exactly the direction where I'm pointing (the barn, ostensibly). Then someone backstage makes a really loud "BACAW!" chicken noise, and that's pretty much the end of the end.

The audience is screaming with laughter, especially when the fan gets turned off and the damned beard/chicken lands on the bride's veil. She ends up holding it along with her bouquet for the duration of the scene, which no one hears anyway because of the laughing.

It is very, very bad.

34

Luckily, pretty much everyone I know came on opening night. So as I'm slinking out once the show finally staggers to a halt, I figure I can escape without seeing anyone.

Wrong, as usual.

The first person I see is Julie Nelson, who looks even more pissed off than Ned, if that's possible. She clomps over to me and shrieks, "How *could* you? You *destroyed* Ned's closing performance! You little . . . aauuuugggh! Trust me, Finkelstein, you'll never be in another show again!"

Oh, no. What a heartbreaker. Believe me, the second the beard landed on Tzeitel, I started weighing Astronomy Club versus Lit Mag as next year's spring activity. For once, Julie's threats don't scare me at all.

Her eyebrows still do, though. And yet . . .

"Wow, Julie. I had no idea you had so much pull with the theater department. Have you also considered running for mayor of New York?"

Holy crap. Did I just say that out loud?

From the look of outrage on Julie's face, it's apparent that I did. *Is she going to kick me in the head?* Nope. She just starts sputtering unintelligibly and then spins on her heel and leaves in a huff.

Amazing! I feel like a million bucks!

As Julie storms off, Lexi comes running up. "Wow, Kelsey, that was—well, it was different than the Broadway version. Way to make the part your own. Nice beard, uh, thing."

And now I'm back to three bucks. Oh, well.

"Thanks, Lex. Thanks a ton."

"At least you won't have to worry about that happening in real life. I mean, unless you develop a hormonal problem. Or move to a farm. Ha."

I'm about to throw myself down a hole and pull the dirt in after me when suddenly the image of what the beard flying around must have looked like to the audience comes to me . . . and I burst out laughing. Lexi starts laughing. Soon we're both practically crying, leaning against the wall. Through peals of laughter, Lexi gasps, "When it flew up . . . the chickens . . . the chickens . . ."

"Oh, God," I wheeze. "I told you it was going to be a complete disas—"

Then I feel a tap on my shoulder. I wipe my eyes and sort of snuffle in my last guffaw as I turn around . . .

Of course. It's Ben. Ben . . . and Valentina, the girl with the funky glasses from the terrible party—his girlfriend, obviously. Perfect.

Ben looks extremely cute and highly amused, which makes me want to run as fast as I can to Antarctica. Sadly, that isn't an option, so instead I say, "Oh, hey. Thanks for coming to the show. Uh, you know Lexi." I turn to her. "Lex, this is, um—"

"Val," she says, holding out her hand imperiously. She's got the other hand on Ben's arm. Okay, we get it. He's all yours. Geez.

"Hey, Val." Lexi gives her a lazy, dismissive smile that no one else could ever pull off. "So, Ben, what'd you think of the show? Kelsey was pretty great, huh?"

Ben laughs. "Yeah. I didn't know it was gonna be a comedy, though."

"Well, I'm all about, um, keeping things, you know, fresh." *Shut up, Kelsey!* "So, how's the paper? Ruin any lives lately besides mine?" *Better. Now stop talking immediately.*

"Hey, speaking of the paper—Lexi, aren't you supposed to be writing an article on the play? You should be getting quotes and stuff. Bad reporter!" Ben scolds her, his eyes all twinkly and crinkly and—

Hey! Stop thinking he is cute at once! This guy saw you at your absolute saddest moment, alone in a dark bedroom. Remember?

"Oh, yeah, that's true." Lexi is nodding. "So, Ms. Finkelstein, can I get a quote about tonight's performance? Any thoughts for our readers?"

"Yeah . . . I think I'd rather not say what I thought about tonight's performance. Ask Ned for a quote—I'm sure he has *plenty* to say. You'll find him crying on Julie Nelson's shoulder," I add, pointing to our star.

Lexi glances over at them. "I don't know if I feel like getting my eyes clawed out tonight. Hey, you're friends with Julie, aren't you?" she asks, turning to Valentina. "Any chance I could get you to smooth the way for me?"

Um, Lexi? Whatcha doing there, lady?

Valentina looks totally disarmed. "Uh, what?" She looks at Ben. "Weren't we gonna go to—"

"Of course she will. Val, this is a budding reporter here. You can help her out, can't you?"

Valentina grudgingly disentangles herself from Ben and starts walking toward Julie and Ned. Lexi winks at me, following in her wake. What is she *doing*?

Ben and I stand alone in the hallway uncomfortably.

"So . . . ," I manage. "Thanks again for coming. Did you, uh, enjoy the show? I mean, before it fell apart in a fiery blaze of horror?"

"I think that was the best part, actually. You should definitely consider a professional career."

"Ha ha. And to reiterate . . . ha."

God, this is awkward.

I sort of hope it lasts forever.

"So, hey—you never got back to me about the special-delivery paper I snagged for you. Is that any way to show supreme gratitude?"

I'm sorry—what? "Gratitude?!" I squeak. "It was a terrible picture! What was I supposed to be grateful for, exactly?"

Ben looks genuinely nonplussed. "What are you talking about? It was a *great* picture; you looked totally psyched in it about getting your award. I thought you'd like it! No?"

Okay, now *I'm* confused. "Ben. I'm missing a tooth in that picture."

"What? No you aren't."

I laugh. "Uh, yeah, I totally am."

"But . . . I saw you that afternoon and your teeth were fine."

"Yeah, 'cause I'd just gotten back from the dentist. Do you know how much crap I got for that picture?" *What is going on here?*

"Man . . . I guess I didn't look at it that carefully. When it was submitted, I mean. We just go through the thumbnails and choose . . . man, I'm sorry. Now I feel bad." He actually looks like he feels bad.

Now *I* feel sort of bad.

"It's fine—I'm used to it by now. Seriously, it's cool. But, um, what exactly do you *do* for the paper, anyway?" I ask, starting to get just a *tiny* bit suspicious. "I thought you said Kate Izzo chose—"

"Well, that was fun." Valentina saunters over and links her arm through Ben's. "Ned is *such* a drama queen. Lexi had a few more questions, but I told her we were running late, so . . . you ready to go?"

"Uh, yeah," Ben says. He puts his arm around Valentina and gives her one of his crinkly-eyed grins. Then he turns back to me. "Well, sorry again about the picture. I honestly thought you'd be pleased."

"No, it's really okay."

Valentina is looking at me in a not-very-friendly way now.

Uncomfortable pause? Paging uncomfortable pause? Come in, please!

Finally, Ben goes, "Okay, cool. Well, great job. See you." He turns to go, but then stops. "Um, Kelsey . . . I also wanted to say—and I know this is none of my business, but . . ." *Oh, please, no. What now?* "I hope you aren't getting involved with Sam Sharpe. He's kind of a—"

"Ben!" Valentina hisses, poking him in the side. "Don't embarrass her!"

"Sorry. It's just, you know, he can seem really—"

"No, no, I know!" I blurt out, rapid-fire. "Nothing going on there, not to worry!" *I am going to die of humiliation. This is it—I am going to actually expire, right now, right here, with leftover glue on my face.*

"Ben, let's gooooo!" Valentina tugs his arm, shooting me a pitying smile. Fortunately, Em, JoJo, and Cass have finally come out of the theater and they're all keyed up. I gratefully let them drag me away to the cast party, leaving

Ben and Val and my dignity and my fat suit and everything else behind.

Show over, just like that.

The cast party is a super heap of fun, if you consider watching a bunch of other people making out and/or reenacting the flying beard catastrophe to be a heap of fun. Also Ned, who seems to have mostly recovered, makes a big speech about how much we all mean to him and that when he's at Northwestern next year we're all welcome to visit him and experience theater at a "college level." (Goody gumdrops. Pardon my elbows as I shove to the front of the line for that choice opportunity.)

I mostly spend the night exchanging "You were amazing!"s, hugging everyone, signing people's scripts and/or programs for scrapbook purposes, avoiding Julie's evil eye(brows), helping collect discarded cups, and trying to pretend my entire post-play conversation with Ben didn't happen. Especially the part where he gave me dating advice in front of his hot girlfriend.

I'm thinking this is an ideal time to go home and start researching the convent system.

35

I'm in my room after dinner, three incredibly dull weeks after the Great Beard Escape. Now that the play's over, I don't really have anything to do except study. Which is boring. I mean, I have my friends, obviously, but they're all studying, too. I'm trying to understand why I need to re-create Euclid's constructions. I mean, they didn't even have toilet paper when he invented these. And everyone wore mandals. Is this really relevant?

Thankfully, my phone buzzes with a text from Lexi, and it says: PROM! CALL ME ASAP!

Huh?

Well, that's a hell of a lot more interesting than math homework. I dial Lexi's number.

"That was fast!"

"You said ASAP! What can I say? I take direction extremely well. So . . . what's going on?"

"Well, you know how Robby asked me to the junior prom?"

"Of course."

"Well, I said yes."

"That was very kind of you. But do take a second to think of the ten devastated guys who will now have to give up hope, okay? It's the least you can do."

Lexi giggles. "Kelsey, you are too much, seriously."

"Yes, I've been told that before. So that's awesome! But what do you need from yours truly?"

"Well, you know Robby's friend Josh?"

"Uh . . . is he the one with the lisp?"

"No, that's Jon, and it's not a lisp. He had a tongue ring . . . situation. Anyway, no. Josh is the one with the longish curly hair? He plays lacrosse? He used to date Zoe Walls?"

"Okay, yeah, I think so. And?"

"*And,* they broke up. See, he thought she was flirting with this guy she knew from another school when she was at his game last week, so he hooked up with this girl Camilla Toht, who graduated last year—"

"Do I know her?"

"Probably not. Anyway, so they hooked up and it turned out that Zoe didn't even—"

I sense this is going to be a very long and complicated tale about two or more people I barely know. "Wait, wait, hang on. I'm getting lost here," I interrupt.

"Right, sorry," Lexi says. "Anyway, it doesn't matter. The

point is, now Josh needs a prom date and Robby asked me if I had a friend he could go with and . . . I said you! Won't that be fun?"

"Wait. What?"

"You're going to the prom! It's at the Mandarin Oriental and we're going to get a limo. Oh, and the after party is at—"

"Lex, hang on—why would this Josh guy want to take me to prom? Does he even know who I am?"

"Well, he wasn't sure, and he didn't see the play . . ."

"Thank God!"

"So I showed him that picture I have of you on my phone, you know, the one of us after soccer practice?"

"Oh my God, you did not! Why didn't you just show him the one of me with the cafeteria workers from *The Reflector*? Jesus, Lexi!"

"And he thought you were *super cute,* which you are, and he said he was sick of dealing with the obnoxious girls in his class, so he wants you to go with him! Isn't that great?"

I take a second to mull this over. I mean, going to the junior prom as a freshman? Extremely cool. Definitely in keeping with my (thus far, not what I'd intended) plan to have an outstanding freshman year of high school. I guess it's not *quite* the scenario I would've come up with, i.e., being actually *asked* by a guy who liked me instead of tagging along as a date replacement. But hey, you can't have everything in this life, right?

Lexi is still making plans on the other end of the line. "You'll need to get a dress! And your mom will let you get your hair done, right? Then we can get ready together. And—"

"Lex, Lex, slow down. Yes, it will definitely be really fun. And seriously, it was so sweet of you to think of me."

"Kels, we're gonna have such a great time. Maybe you and Josh will hit it off! And if not, there will be lots of cute boys there. Including . . . a certain junior named Ben?"

Oh, lordy. Lexi has not let up on the Ben theme since, well, the day we both met him in the paper office. If I let her, she'll go into a detailed story right now of how he's going to leave his date (Val, I'm sure) behind on the dance floor for me. Which will only get my hopes up and then dash them against the rocks when it doesn't happen.

Not that I like the guy. I'm done with men, as I've stated. Seriously.

"Okay, Lex, I actually have to finish this Euclid stuff. It's for tomorrow, so . . ."

"Fine, fine. Anyway, I'll tell Robby to tell Josh you're in. 'Kay?"

"Sounds good. Thanks!"

And that's that. I guess I'm going to the junior prom!

After I call Em, Cass, and JoJo to tell them the big news, I go down to the kitchen and grab a box of Cinnamon Life from the snack closet. I go into the TV room, where Travis is splayed out on her hideous pink beanbag chair, watching a

Friends rerun. I put down the cereal box and she picks it up and takes a handful. We munch silently for a minute and then I decide I'll try to initiate a sisterly discussion. I say, "Hey, Trav? Do you think about boys yet?"

"Duh, stupid, I have a boyfriend. His name is David D. and we've been going out for three weeks."

Gee. That cheers me right up.

I snatch the Life and go back up to my room. Of course, I had a "boyfriend" when I was ten, too. He's probably asking someone to ask someone else he doesn't know to go to the prom with him right now. Stupid boys. I fish my math homework out of the trash. Stupid Euclid.

Sometimes my life is simply too exhausting to bear.

At school the next day, Cass helpfully points out Josh to me in the hallway. He's pretty cute in a Team Jacob way—and a totally different guy than I thought. But whatever.

"So, am I supposed to, you know . . . introduce myself to him? Or just . . . appear on prom night, or what?"

Cass chews on her hair thoughtfully. "I guess you could go over to him. But what would you say?"

"I dunno—'I'm Kelsey, I don't have a dress yet, but I promise not to show up to your prom naked'?"

JoJo appears beside me. "That's probably the last thing he wants to hear. What else ya got?"

"I don't know. But, I mean, isn't this a little weird? To go to a prom with a guy I've never even spoken to? Shouldn't he be approaching *me*?"

"Welcome to the age of the modern man, Kels," JoJo quips. "If you don't like it, you'd better get out now." I glance at Cassidy, who shrugs. Since the play ended, JoJo has been a bit MIA, and Cass and Em and I are wondering if maybe she's been occupying her time with something we don't know about. As in, a girl. I wish she'd talk to us about it.

Cass goes off to her English class and JoJo and I head to math. On the way in, we pass Keith Mayhew leaving. He gives me a big grin. "Oh, hey, Kelsey! I meant to ask, y'know, what are you doing this weekend?"

The bell rings again and he gets swallowed up in the mass exodus to class. "I'll text you later!" I hear through the melee. JoJo and I exchange a knowing look. Keith's been getting all "Remember when we went to that concert?" with me the last few weeks, trying to convince me to hang out with him again. Well, he can keep his floppy tongue and "comitment" issues to himself, I say.

It is interesting to think about how very, very far away that concert seems, though. And how different things were—*so* much has changed since then. When I planned to have this super memorable freshman year, I had very different kinds of memorable experiences in mind. For instance, none of them involved being goalie, fake beards, friend breakups, terrible make-out experiences, bitchy juniors with giant eyebrows, or being shadowed by a mysterious newspaper photographer.

But . . . now I'm going to the *prom*. Maybe this is the experience I've been waiting for. Maybe the rest of that stuff was just a lead-up to the *real* awesomeness that is headed my way!

All I need now is a dress.

36

"Do you have any idea what things cost, young lady? If you think I get up at six o'clock in the morning to go to work so I can throw money away on crap that's going to fall apart in five minutes, then you've got another think coming. Here's an idea—why don't *you* get a job? Then you can feel free to shop wherever you damn well please."

Well, that experiment was an epic FAIL.

My mother, who was initially elated by the news of my impending prom attendance, was less pleased by the reveal that I hadn't actually been *asked* by anyone, and fell apart completely when I told her where I wanted to shop for a dress. Which is: anywhere but where *she* wants to take me. Which is Loehmann's. Of course.

I decide to run to my room and slam the door, which is as Typically Adolescent as it gets and therefore acceptable, I guess. Life is easier when you know what's expected of you, isn't it? I speed-dial Em.

"Hey, so: disaster. Ma Finkelstein is on the rampage."

"Uh-oh. Is she doing the 'I get up at six o'clock in the morning' routine?"

"Yep," I confirm, turning the volume up on my stereo. "She just got to the part about me getting a job when I split."

"Oh, no! So, what now? You have to get a dress! I'd lend you the one I wore to my cousin's sweet sixteen last year, but . . ."

"But it would drag on the floor behind me by about a foot?"

Em giggles. "Well. Yeah. And I don't think trains are in this year."

I groan despairingly. "I know—I'll just wear the tempting blazer and beautiful checked pants I got on the September Loehmann's trip! I'll probably get asked to dance by every guy there."

"Look, Kels, you have to restrategize. Tell you what— *I'll* go with you to Loehmann's. There has to be *something* normal there. Right?"

"No. It's hopeless."

"Come on," she coaxes in her best soothing voice. "We'll go together. Just us. What do you say?"

"Well . . ."

"Good, it's decided! Now . . . do you think your mom will give you her credit card if you swear to only use it at Loehmann's?"

"Maybe you'd better ask," I sigh. "She likes you a lot more than she likes me."

Saturday afternoon, I follow Em into the store, armed with my mother's credit card and a resolve made of steel (which is instantly penetrated by the sight of two women arguing over what appears to be a pair of high-waisted purple leggings). Immediately, I want to run out. We are the youngest people here by about a generation, and there is a large sign advertising a sale on "Intimates." Kill me.

"Come on," Em says. "We'll go to the dress section. They have lots of designer stuff, I swear!"

"Maybe I should just cancel this whole thing," I grumble as we trudge up about seventeen escalators. "I mean, it's not like Josh even knows me. Lexi can find him someone else. You could go!"

Em holds up a scary pink item and looks at it thoughtfully. "Are you insane?!" I cry. "That has weird fringe all over it! You're supposed to be helping!"

"Kels, it's Oscar de la Renta!"

"It's gross and no way."

"Fiiiine." She puts it back and moves on to the next section. "Anyway . . . I actually can't go to prom with Josh. Because . . . guess who IMed me last night after I hung up with you?" Em leads me over to a rack filled with terrifying gowns. She starts flipping the hangers aside like a seasoned shopper on a mission. I try on a hilarious fur hat and dance around in front of a wall mirror.

"Who?"

"James."

"What?" I stop mid-jig. "What did he say? You should've ignored him—or better, signed off immediately!"

"I know I should've . . . he was such a jerk to me. And the last month or so, I've actually felt like flirting with other guys again. But . . . I couldn't do it. I still miss him so much, Kels. And . . . he apologized. *A lot.*"

"Hmph." I scowl, unconvinced. I hold up a relatively plain, long violet dress. "How about this?"

"I think that's a nightgown," Em whispers, doing a weird thing with her eyes. I look in the direction she's indicating and see a saleslady sneering at us from across the store. Terrific. Just what I need—a hovering Loehmann's employee. I put the nightgown back on the rack.

"Em, I know you miss him. And I'm glad he apologized . . . but now what happens?"

"Well, he asked for another chance and swore he wouldn't hurt me again. He wants to make plans to see each other before the summer."

"Em . . ."

"He's matured a lot in the last six months!"

"He's fourteen—how much could he have matured? Has his voice even changed yet?"

"Actually, yes." Em blushes. "And he's fifteen now, anyway. We Skyped last night. For, like, two hours. It was so nice. . . ."

She trails off, smiling dreamily at an absolutely hideous one-shouldered affair, which apparently retails for $1800. She looks so happy. And why shouldn't she be happy? She's the nicest person on the planet, for crying out loud. I decide to be happy for her. But this James guy better watch it—I'll take him *out* if he disappoints her again, and that's a fact.

"This is the one!" Em cries, holding up a dress. I cover my eyes and peer through my fingers like she's showing me a scary movie. I'm ready to be horrified. And it's . . . actually, it's not awful at all. It's a silky fabric in a pretty sky blue color, with a scooped neckline, spaghetti straps, and an empire waist. I check the tag. Within the budget! I seriously can't believe I found a normal dress at Loehmann's. And no one will know where it came from but me, Em, and my mother's credit card company.

What feels like a thousand hours later, Em and I get back to my house. I've got a dress, shoes, a necklace, and a head-ache. Em has six new texts from James and a happy heart. Success all around.

We haul ourselves up to my room and I hang the dress in the closet. It really is very nice, and I actually like how I look in it. Maybe prom will turn out to be fun?

My phone rings, and it's JoJo. "What're you up to?" she asks.

"Em and I just got back to my house. I got a dress!"

"Awesome. Can Cass and I come over? We're bored."

"Yeah, of course. See you soon."

I hang up and find Em texting away. "You aren't going to start this again, are you? Make yourself unavailable! He hasn't earned your undivided attention back," I remonstrate.

"You're right!" she says, snapping the phone shut and stuffing it in her bag. She flops onto the floor, stretching out. "I love shopping! I'm so glad we found you something. Do you think maybe you and Josh will hook up?"

"Ugh, I don't know. I haven't had the best luck in that department so far this year, as you may recall. Two total failures in the makeout department," I sigh, sitting next her on the carpet. "And don't bad things happen in threes? Maybe I shouldn't chance it."

"I dunno, Kels. It is *prom*. Very romantic."

"I wish you and Cass and JoJo were going to be there, too. I mean, I love Lexi, but she'll be with Robby and I won't really know anyone else except Jill from the play and, of course, Julie Nelson. And she'll probably chuck her dinner roll at me."

"Well, if she's as lousy at baseball as she is at soccer, you're safe."

"Good point."

"*Ben* will be there," Em says, rolling over and batting her eyelashes at me.

"Don't you start! Lexi is bad enough. I don't know where

you guys get this stuff from. I don't even *know* the guy, *and* he has a girlfriend . . . and there's something sketchy about him, anyway. There is no reason for you to bug me about him!"

"Well, there wouldn't be . . . except you totally like him. It's *so* obvious."

"How can it be obvious? You've never even seen us in the same room together—and no, a hallway doesn't count. *And* he walked in on me at one of the worst moments of my life. *And* he's totally conceited. *And*—"

"Methinks you protest too much!" JoJo announces, sashaying through my bedroom door.

"That's *not* the line." Cass follows behind her.

"Whatever." JoJo sticks her tongue out at Cass. Cass returns the favor.

"Very mature, ladies." Em giggles. The girls throw their stuff in the corner and pull up some floor space.

"The point is," JoJo continues, "*I* saw you talking to him at rehearsal. He pushes your buttons. You love that."

"My mom pushes my buttons, and I hate it."

"So not the same thing," Cass says. "I think he likes you back. Otherwise, why would he go out of his way to flirt with you all the time?"

"Teasing is not *always* flirting—"

JoJo jumps in. "He gave you that newspaper with your picture from the awards thing—that means he was thinking about you. Even if it turned out, uh—"

"Horrifying?" I suggest.

"—less than desirable," JoJo says. "He meant it nicely. I mean, he told you that."

"Yeah, right before he brought up the Sam thing! And this was all weeks ago, anyway. Totally irrelevant. I've barely seen him since then."

Okay, that's not *totally* true. I've run into him in the hall at school a bunch of times, but I always find an excuse to escape when he starts a conversation. I just get so flustered around him.

"You guys are bonkers. Besides, even if he did like me, which he doesn't—and have we forgotten about his girlfriend, by the way?—I don't like him back. He's . . . too . . . you know. Something annoying," I sum up grandly.

"Kels. Come on. You can tell *us*! I think we've *all* learned this year," JoJo says, raising her eyebrow at Cass, who blushes, "that honesty is the best policy. Right?"

Em and I exchange a look. Was that a meaningful segue or not? I prepare myself to be extremely supportive just in case. I say, "Of course. We should all feel completely able to tell each other anything. If it's true, that is," I add (just to clarify that I'm *not* talking about Ben).

"Definitely. What's the point otherwise?" Cass agrees. She gives me a smile.

"Well, James and I made up. So . . . that happened," Em volunteers, getting the ball rolling. Cass and JoJo gasp excitedly, and Em fills them in on the details.

Then: "So . . . since we're in sharing mode, I actually wanted to talk to you guys about something," JoJo says tentatively.

Oh my God. Is she going to come out to us? Finally? Should we act surprised or go straight for the supportive thing?

"You've probably noticed I haven't been around so much lately," she goes on, "and I wanted to explain that, um . . . well, it's not because I don't want to hang with you guys. Obviously."

"Obviously!" Em squeaks. JoJo gives her an odd look. I give her a surreptitious poke.

"So . . . yeah, anyway, I've just kind of been dealing with some, um . . . See, this year I realized that—well, actually I didn't *realize*, I just, um . . . Well, okay. I met this—"

The door suddenly swings open and bangs against the wall. Travis, in her ridiculous Annie costume, is standing there with her hands on her hips. "Mom wants to know how many people are staying for dinner, because we're having pizza!"

I scramble to my feet and haul her out of the doorway and into the hall. She starts shrieking immediately.

"Mom!" I holler as I stomp down the stairs, still dragging Travis. "Can you *please* not let her come barging into my room like that? Is it too much to ask for some *privacy* in my own house?"

My mother comes out of the kitchen drying her hands

on a dishcloth. "First of all, this is *my* house, not yours—so yes, it is. Second, let go of your sister." She looks over at Travis. "And you: stop being a pest."

I release Travis, who makes a dash for the TV room. "Mom. Seriously? You guys couldn't have stopped at one? For the world's sake, if not mine?" I turn, disgusted, and head back up the stairs. "We're four for dinner," I call over my shoulder. "And *no olives*!"

I get back to my room and slam the door. Dealing with this family is beyond my capabilities, honestly. I may soon be unable to soldier on.

Unfortunately, the intense conversation window has clearly closed now. I sit back down with the girls and apologize for the interruption, but JoJo waves it aside and says it was no big deal. Stupid Travis! If JoJo's budding sexuality is stunted by the antics of a part-time Annie, I will have to behead her.

"Okay, you guys!" I say, trying to break the tension. "We're getting pizza! And . . . I'm going to prom with Josh, um, Something, who is a cute and *available* junior that I might feel like making out with! Let's talk about him, shall we?"

So we do.

37

I may not make it to prom after all. I might be in jail for killing my mother. She is driving me up the wall, into the sky, onto the sun, and out of the solar system.

She *refused* to let me get ready at Lexi's house, even though now she has to drive me there so the limo doesn't have to make an extra stop. She insisted that she wanted to see me all dressed up and have a real "mother-daughter" moment. I finally acquiesced, since it took me a whole day already to explain to her why my date was meeting me at Lexi's and not picking me up in a horse and carriage like in the olden days.

She did let me go to a salon with Lexi to get my hair done this afternoon at least. She drew the line at fabulous blond highlights, though, which was Typical Lame Parent Behavior as far as *I'm* concerned. But my hair does look really good—the guy blew it out super-straight and it feels really swingy and full. I just hope it doesn't get all stringy before I even get there from repeated hair-flipping on my part. I just can't help it!

So now I'm made up, bejeweled, heeled, dressed, and ready to go. I think I look good. I hope Josh thinks so. I mean, this is kind of a "take it or leave it" situation for him, but it would be great if he didn't puke when he saw me heading his way. I don't think the old self-esteem could handle that, frankly.

Deep breath. I grab the silk wrap and beaded clutch Mom lent me and head down to the living room. I practically fall down the stairs when my dad blinds me with his camera but manage not to end up in a heap at the foot of the staircase. A neck brace would really *not* complete my ensemble.

"Oh, Kelsey . . . you look like a *WOMAN*!" my mother exclaims. *Gross. Can we not say things like that in front of Dad, please? Or at all?*

"Thanks, Mom. So . . . can we go?"

"Just a few more pictures—and you'd better get some with your date! I still can't believe he didn't come over here to introduce himself, by the way. When I was your age—"

"Right, yes, I know. But seriously, things have changed since the invention of electricity. So . . . can we wrap this up?"

"Watch it, Kelsey. Just because I'm glowing with maternal pride at the moment doesn't mean I can't ground you for the rest of your life starting right now."

Argh. Where is my Typical Adolescent leeway when I need it most?

"Sorry, but I'm nervous! My hair might get stringy. And I don't want to be late."

"Come on, honey, you look terrific," my dad says, hauling out a scary camera attachment that will probably burn my skin off. "Just a couple more pics, huh? Stand with your mom over there near the mantel."

Sigh.

A hundred years later, we finally leave. Miraculously, my mother gets an emergency phone call from my sister just as we pull up to Lexi's house. Apparently, she can't find her Annie costume (could someone have hidden it behind the washing machine? I wonder . . .) and Mom is therefore unable to hang around and embarrass me in front of my date. Pity, that.

Josh looks really cute in his tux. He stands by stoically with Robby while Lexi and I hug and shriek over each other's outfits. Lexi, in a strapless silvery sheath of a gown and her hair curled halfway down her back, looks like she just wandered off the cover of *Elle*. But I actually feel pretty good about myself tonight, even in comparison.

"You look nice," Josh says. His voice is much deeper than I expected, which is a tad disconcerting. I don't know if I'm prepared to slow dance with Voldemort tonight.

"Thanks. And thanks for inviting me, by the way," I say breezily, like this is the fifth prom I've been to this month. I even manage to pin on the boutonniere my mother insisted I bring for him without stabbing either of us. Success!

"You guys want some champagne?" Lexi asks, holding up an open bottle.

"Nah, I'm sticking with herbal tonight," Josh says. He pulls a little ceramic pipe that looks like a regular cigarette from the inside pocket of his coat jacket. "It's a one-hitter," he explains when he sees me looking. "You want? I've got plenty."

"Uh, no, thanks, I'm fine with—"

"Josh, you can't smoke that in my house!" Lexi interjects. "My parents will freak if they smell it. Anyway, I don't want my dress to reek of pot."

"Fine, whatever. I can wait till we get there." Josh tucks the little pipe back in his jacket. He shoves his hands in the pockets of his tuxedo pants and rocks back and forth on the balls of his feet, staring at the ceiling. Then he gazes at the floor for a while. *Is he already high, or is he just really boring? Or both?* I sip my champagne and smother a giggle when Lexi rolls her eyes at me.

Robby downs his champagne in one gulp and sets the glass on the coffee table. "So . . . should we head?"

"Wait! I promised my mom I'd get a picture of all of us!" I grab my digital camera from my purse. One plus about being with guys who barely speak: I don't bother feeling dumb when I say dorky things about pictures for my mom. Who cares?

260

Lexi's dad comes in and takes pictures of the four of us in every combination possible. My mother will be simply delighted with the shots of me and Josh (who I've now discerned is definitely somewhat stoned as well as dumber than a box of hair) standing awkwardly next to each other. Then we pile into the limo, stop to pick up the rest of our group—two other guys from the lacrosse team and their dates—and head to the dance.

When we pull up to the hotel, it's totally gorgeous and all lit up and I start to get really excited and nervous for no particular reason. The guys flash our invitations to the doormen and we go up in the elevator, exiting into a beautiful ballroom all decorated in black and white. (It's not until later that I realize the theme is actually "The Intrigue of Chess," which is weird and makes no sense at all. Who was on this prom committee, anyway? And what could the rejected suggestions possibly have been? Bunions? Gang Warfare? But I digress.) We find our table, put down our wraps, and Lexi and I head for the bathroom immediately to check our makeup. Of course, when we get there, it's full of girls.

"Lex," I say quietly. "You didn't tell me Josh was a total pothead! If I go home smelling like weed, my mother will actually kill me. Not like yours—but real, actual *death*."

"I know, sorry—they sort of all are, and I forgot you don't smoke. But he won't do it here. I mean, there are teachers and stuff! He's a bit dim, but not *that* dumb." Lexi whips out some shimmery lip gloss and a little brush and starts applying it carefully.

"Yeah, about that—"

"Oh my God. How did *you* get in here?" I turn and there she is—Ms. Julie Nelson herself, surrounded by her friends. Of course I knew she'd be here, but I didn't think I'd run into her in the first ten minutes. *Do not panic. She can't do anything to you. She's just a mean, scary girl. Remember how well you handled her after the play?*

"Oh, hey, Julie," I say, trying to sound friendly. "I'm here with Josh, uh—"

"Just don't get in my way, Finkelstein. This is *my* prom, not yours." She fluffs her hair in the mirror, then turns back. "Hi, Lexi. Hot dress."

And she stomps out with her friends in tow.

"Well, that went remarkably well!" I say to Lexi with false cheer.

"Whatever, Kels—just ignore her. You are awesome and she's just insecure." Lexi scoops up her makeup and crams it back in her purse. "Ready?"

"Let's roll," I say. We head for the door.

When we get back to the ballroom, Robby is sitting at our table with one of the other girls we came with. He looks up excitedly when Lexi approaches—though, to be fair, so does every other guy in the place. Josh, the other two lacrosse players, and one of their dates are nowhere in sight. I sit down and start flexing my toes, which already hurt inside my new shoes, when Jill, who played Golde in *Fiddler,* slides into the seat next to me.

"You look fantastic!" she gushes. "Where's your date?"

"Hey! You look great, too—I *love* your eye makeup. And I have no idea where my date is, actually. Hey, Robby," I say, leaning across the table. "Where's Josh, do you know?"

"Oh, yeah, he and the guys went out for a smoke. They'll be back in a sec, prob'ly," Robby offers. I see some movement under the table and realize he's pouring something from a flask into his glass of Coke. *Sweet.*

I'm contemplating how to get in on that when Dr. Shanman, the scary math teacher and one of the chaperones, approaches the table. She looks mad. She also appears to be wearing a burgundy bedspread, belted around the middle with a kind of weird sash. I *think* it's meant to be a dress of some sort. At least she took off her customary leather fanny pack for the occasion.

"Robert Amabile!" she bellows, totally drowning out Jay-Z's latest dance remix. "Do you know where your teammates are?"

Robby's head snaps up. His hands are still underneath the table. Oh, God. This is not good. "Uh . . . yeah, I think they had to make a phone call."

"Really, all of them together? How interesting."

"Uhhhh . . ."

"I think Steve had to make a call and the others went, too, Dr. Shanman. Is everything okay?" Lexi interjects smoothly. Man, she is good under pressure. I glance at Jill, who looks as freaked out as I feel.

"No, young lady, it is not." She lowers her voice and speaks in a dangerously dark tone. "Your friends have been escorted off the premises for smoking marijuana, which as I'm sure you are aware is *illegal* and, obviously, expressly forbidden at school functions. Now, since you four are still in the ballroom, I will assume that blah blah blah . . ."

Oh. My. God.

Seriously? We've been here for fifteen minutes and my date has already been kicked out and possibly arrested? This is very bad. Am I in trouble by association? I've never even *tried* pot! But I had a glass of champagne at Lexi's. What if they do a Breathalyzer test? What if Shanman makes Robby stand up right now and she finds his flask and he's kicked off the lacrosse team and we're all roped together and tossed in the Hudson River?!

I guess this means I'm not going to get a prom portrait taken with Josh tonight. My mom is not going to like that one bit.

38

We do not get arrested. Dr. Shanman harangues us about surrounding ourselves with the right kind of people in the future and then stalks off to go write a report about half the lacrosse team, who were all caught and will probably not be playing a whole lot of lacrosse the last month of school.

Once Shanman left, Robby practically hyperventilated about his close call; the only reason he wasn't out there with Josh and the others is because Lexi had gotten so pissed off at him when he pulled the same stunt at the winter formal that he decided to hold off till after dinner to ditch her and go get high. A real romantic, Robby is. Lexi seems to appreciate the gesture, though, as she is now comforting him with a great deal of gusto and smearing of lip gloss on the dance floor.

Jill excused herself to fill her friends in on the exciting scandal, so I sit with Jen—the other now-dateless girl at my table—and try to find something to talk about. Turns out the only thing we have in common is that we are both sitting alone at the prom.

I hate to say it, but so far? Prom blows.

I grab my cell phone and step outside the ballroom to call Em. She picks up after one ring.

"Hi! So, how's it going? Do you like Josh? Does everyone love your dress?"

"Em. You are not going to believe what is happening over here. It's insane, even for me."

I quickly fill her in. When I wrap up the pot saga, she asks, "So, you're just at the prom by yourself now?"

"Uh, sort of, yeah. I mean, Lexi is here, obviously, but she's with Robby. And then there's the effervescent Julie Nelson, who I think would rather be stuffed inside a suitcase with a scorpion than take me under her wing for the evening."

"Should I call JoJo and Cass? Maybe we can—"

"Well, look who it is," a familiar voice behind me cuts in. I can practically feel Ben's ironic grin before I even see it.

"Sorry, Em—I'll call you back, okay?" I hang up and turn around.

Oh, man. Ben looks really, really hot in a tuxedo. Valentina is with him, of course, wearing a beautiful vintage dress that fits her perfectly and different glasses than usual—these have tiny rhinestones on the sides. They both look glamorous and perfect and suddenly I feel like Travis playing dress-up in my mom's clothes.

Okay, fine. I will admit it. I totally have a crush on Ben.

Which is why I have to get out of here immediately.

266

"Hey, Ben. Hey, Val, uh . . . you guys look amazing. I mean, I'd love to chat, but I have to, uh, go find Lexi because, you know, we, uh . . . came together. So. Yeah."

"Hang on a sec—where's your date? Didn't you come with Josh Ostfeld?"

How did he know that? Is it possible Ben *has* been keeping tabs on me?

"Oh, yeah, Josh. Uh, he got arrested. I think. I don't know, actually, but he was definitely removed from the premises." Good, that's great. Now they know you're here without a date. *Why don't you just print up invitations to your pity party and call it a night?*

"Arrested? You're kidding, right?" Valentina looks stunned. Then she bursts into peals of laughter. "Pay up!" she commands, turning to Ben and holding her hand out, palm up. "I told you someone would get kicked out in the first hour. God, the guys in our class are such *tools.*"

She turns back to me. "Thanks, Kelsey—you just made my night!" She puts her hand on Ben's arm and squeezes it affectionately. "Babe, I've gotta go find Zoe and dish. See you in there, okay?" Then she gathers up her awesome full skirt and heads into the ballroom.

This would be a perfect time for Ben to say something along the lines of, *Gosh, Kelsey. You look so beautiful, I think I will immediately break up with Val and sweep you off to the Riviera for a romantic weekend. I trust you enjoy bouillabaisse?*

"Kelsey, Kelsey, Kelsey. You really know how to find

trouble, don't you?" Ben's eyes crinkle up as usual. Now I sort of want to punch him.

"Well, I do what I can to keep you entertained, Ben. No need to thank me—it's a totally free service. So, yeah. I've gotta go."

I dash away as fast as I can in my teetering shoes, only glancing back as I'm slipping through the doors of the ballroom. Is it me, or does he look just the tiniest bit perturbed?

Eh. It's probably just me.

When I see that Lexi is now slow-dancing with Robby in a way that definitely does *not* invite interruption, I make an executive decision to head to the bathroom and collect my thoughts.

I stand in front of the sinks and look at myself in the mirror. Ugh. This is a total rerun of the night of the Foreign Scarves concert—me, staring at myself in the mirror, wondering what the hell happened.

I adjust one of the straps on my dress, thinking. This whole year has been ridiculous. First soccer, then fights with my friends, the tragic pictures in the paper, guy disasters, the play . . . it's like I'm some kind of magnet for catastrophe! The plan was to live up to my full potential and be awesome and make the world notice me for a change. Well, they noticed all right. What a nightmare.

I'm thinking that maybe I should just grab my stuff and

hightail it back to Brooklyn where I belong when someone comes out of a stall. Of course: it's Julie Nelson. She's a bit of a mess and very obviously drunk. She was pre-partying before she got here, from the look of it. I wonder where her friends are.

"Uh, Julie? Are you . . . okay?" I ask tentatively.

"Oh my Gooooooooooddddd, why are you following me everywhere? You know, Finkelstein, you think you're so cool, don't you? You just do whatever you want and every-one thinks you're hilarious . . . well, let me tell you—tell *you*—" She blanches and puts her hand over her mouth.

Oh, God. Is she going to puke? I make a move toward her, just in case she needs help.

"I'm *FINE*." She waves me away firmly. "I'm not a fresh-man, you know, I can hold my liquor. And unlike some people, I—oh, God—"

She bends over the sink and starts retching. I quickly flip the lock on the bathroom door and run to pull her hair back. Luckily it's half-up, so she doesn't get anything on it. She's breathing heavily and tears are streaming from her eyes, and I have absolutely no idea what to do other than rub her back and pray she just drank too much and will be fine now that she threw most of it up. I really would love to avoid being connected to more than one group of people getting kicked out of prom, if possible.

I get Julie's purse off the floor of the stall she was in

and fish out her powder compact, which I hand to her. She starts blotting her face with the puff. "You want me to get you some ginger ale or something?" I ask tentatively.

"No, just . . . I'm okay now." Our eyes meet in the mirror. She grabs a tissue and starts wiping away some of the streaked mascara. "Look, I didn't eat much today, that's all." She sniffs and sort of half laughs, half gulps. "You look totally freaked out. Chill, I'm fine."

"Okay. Uh, Julie, your dress is kind of—"

I hear someone knocking on the bathroom door. "Julie? Julie? Are you in there?"

I unlock and open the door. Her friends rush past me and swarm around the sinks. "Oh my God, Jules, are you okay? We were so worried!" They all seem kind of wasted themselves, actually. I hope they can hold each other's hair now, because I would really like to get out of here.

"Guys, I'm fine! Stop fussing at me," Julie snaps. She looks up at me in the mirror again. "Well, Finkelstein? You need something?"

"Uh—nope. No, I'm just going. But, your, um—"

"Great. *Bye*." She gives me a death-ray glare in the mirror. Okay, fine. I can take a hint.

I back out of the bathroom. I can't believe that girl! I help her cover up a vomiting episode and she's *still* a total bitch to me?

I guess it's a shame, really. If only she'd been even a *little* bit nicer, I would've stuck around to tell her that the top of her strapless dress has fallen down and her flesh-colored paste-on bra is totally showing. And she looks *ridiculous*. Not to mention naked.

Oh, well. I'm sure one of her wasted friends will notice.

39

I'm heading to the table to get my wrap, say a quick good-bye to Lexi, and see if I can make it home in time to catch the new *SNL* when I feel my phone vibrating inside my clutch. I take it out and flip it open to see a text from Em. It says, WE'RE HERE! COME TO THE ELEVATOR!

Huh?

I toss my wrap and purse back on the table and make my way through dancing loons until I get to the double doors of the ballroom. I feel like I've walked about twelve miles in these damned heels—and for what? Sigh. I go out to the hallway by the elevator bank. It's empty, of course—everyone arrived by now and went inside. What the heck did Em mean?

I'm about to go back for my phone to call her when the elevator doors open. And there they are, all dressed up: my three besties in the whole frickin' world. Em is wearing the dress from her cousin's sweet sixteen last year. Cass and JoJo are both wearing gowns that may have once belonged to JoJo's mom. They look weird, but fabulous.

"How did you guys get in here?!" I shriek after we have a massive group hug. "You don't have prom invitations—didn't they check?"

"I made a coupla calls," JoJo explains, obviously pleased with herself. "Turns out the concierge used to belong to a nudist colony my parents were into a few years ago. I offered to bring a few pictures with me, and he said not to bother because there'd be no problem at all if we just came on up to meet you. Wasn't that nice?"

"You guys are so, so awesome. I can't believe you came all the way here!"

"Well, we heard you needed a date," Cass says, linking her arm through mine.

"Oh, God. I was just about to leave, actually."

"Kelsey, this is your first prom! You can't leave early!" Em insists. "Besides, have you even danced yet?"

"I haven't done anything yet except march around in these horrible pinchy shoes you made me buy and hold Julie Nelson's hair while she puked. I haven't even had dinner!"

The girls and I go back into the ballroom, toss our stuff down on the empty seats at my table, and hit the dance floor. Five feet away from me, Ned Garman is whispering something in Julie Nelson's ear that, based on the look of horror on his face and her freaked-out reaction, has to be: "Holy shit, your dress fell down! Fix it, quick!"

What a lovely, *lovely* turn the evening has taken.

. . .

After a while, my feet are actually ready to fall off. I leave my friends bouncing around to Beyoncé and limp over to the nearest empty table, plop down in a seat, and slip the horrible heels off. Oh, glorious relief! I help myself to some water. Whoever was sitting here left a gorgeous antique-looking purse on the table. I pick it up to admire it more closely, and the clasp pops open. Crap. A cell phone and lipstick fall out, which I quickly put back inside. The other item is more interesting. It's a digital camera—an expensive-looking one, I see when I take it out of its case. Which normally I wouldn't do, but this particular camera case has a sticker on it. A label, really, that reads, in big letters: Property of The Reflector. Underneath that is a smaller sticker with the school's address in case someone finds it.

Interesting. Very, very interesting.

That's when I notice the prom invitations that were underneath the bag. Of course—it's Val's purse. I should've guessed, since it goes perfectly with her dress. And this invitation must be Ben's. Ben . . . the photographer. And huge *liar*, apparently.

I knew it. I knew it, I knew it, I *knew* it! I'm not sure when exactly I knew it, but I totally did. I can't believe this—where the heck is that jerk?

I get up, not even bothering to put on my shoes, determined to find that sneaky camera jockey and read him the riot act. Giant submission file indeed. Ha—it was him all along! And why? Why would he purposely take all those awful pictures of me? Did Julie Nelson hire him? To reiterate: WHYYYYY??

I don't see him anywhere on the dance floor. He and Val must have stepped outside for a mid-prom makeout party. Well, this time, I won't mind interrupting at *all*, thank you very much!

I march back out through the double doors. There are a few kids and one chaperone on a cell phone, but no Ben or Val. Aha! I hear voices over by the elevators. It must be them. Determined to give that scoundrel Ben a piece of my mind without getting sidetracked for once by his crinkly eyes, or snarky smile, or *anything else,* I march over to them.

There's Valentina. She's smiling and holding hands with someone. That someone is tucking a lock of hair behind Val's ear for her in a very romantic way. But it is definitely not Ben.

It's JoJo.

40

I stop dead in my tracks. JoJo sees me and turns white. Val, who was saying something, trails off and drops JoJo's hand. We all stand there for a second in total silence.

"I, um . . . I'm just gonna go . . . oh, God." Val shoots a worried look at JoJo and bolts past me. JoJo turns to me, looking totally panicked.

"Kels, I, okay, um . . . this is so not . . . well, okay. Um, I'm gay. I wanted to tell you before, but I wasn't sure . . . if . . . Uh, Kelsey?"

I start laughing. I can't help it. I start laughing so hard I can't stop, and I feel terrible because this is supposed to be a serious, important moment, one I've been preparing to be supportive for since the summer, but of all the ways I thought it would happen, this was never even on my radar. I'm laughing so hard that I start to choke, and JoJo has to pound me on the back till I can breathe again. In the middle of her coming-out speech. Brilliant.

I take a deep breath and straighten up. JoJo is looking at me like she's scared of what I'm going to say. Oh, no!

"JoJo," I say quickly, "I'm so sorry I laughed. It's not funny, it's just—we know. I mean, I know, we *all* know— we've been waiting for *you* to tell *us* all year!"

"You have? But . . ." Now a smile is spreading on JoJo's face. "Why didn't you *say anything*? I've been trying to tell you for months!"

"We didn't want to rush you!"

"Oh, for the love of . . . well, so does this mean you're cool with it?"

"JoJo, of course! Don't be ridiculous!"

JoJo slides down the wall and sits on the floor. I do the same. She lets out a huge breath. "I'm so relieved. I mean, I don't know why I thought you wouldn't—I just . . . I don't know. It seems stupid now."

"It's not stupid," I assure her. "It's a big deal. I mean, it isn't, but . . . you know."

"Yeah."

We sit there for a second. Then I say, "Wait a second. So . . . is Val . . . ?"

"Oh my God, Kels, I've wanted to tell you about *that* for ages, too—she's not Ben's girlfriend!"

"Yeah, I sort of figured that out, thanks. So . . . what are they, then?"

"They've been best friends since forever. But I couldn't tell you without, you know . . . but he *really* likes you! He thought you were so cute and funny when you came into the office all pissed off that day . . . I tried to give you hints about it, but you didn't—"

"JoJo, he does *not* like me. This is what I've been trying to tell you the whole time! *He* is the photographer for the paper. I just found his camera and came out here to rip him a new one. He's been taking all those awful pictures of me all year! On purpose!"

"Kels, *no*." JoJo gets serious. "The first ones were totally a coincidence, and he felt really bad, seriously. So then he took that picture of you from the awards assembly and thought you'd be so happy, but he didn't notice the tooth thing . . . he really *was* trying to be nice! And he was so bummed out when he thought you were into that Sam idiot, and he told Val you've been avoiding him since then, and *I* knew it was because you felt dumb, but . . ."

My head is spinning, trying to take this all in. "So, wait. Slow down. When did you meet Valentina? I'm so lost."

"At the party we went to with Lexi. The night you made up with Cass. The night—"

"And all this time you knew? JoJo! I may have to kill you."

"I know, I know, but how do you think I feel? I wanted you to get together with Ben so bad and obviously tell you about my—about Val . . . but—"

"Okay. Okay. So, is that it, then?" I stand up and haul

JoJo to her feet. "Have you told me everything? You aren't also becoming a Buddhist, or a vegan, or a man, or anything else life-changing? Today, anyway?"

"Not that I'm aware of, no."

"Okay, great. In that case . . . I'll see you later."

Then I run for the ballroom doors.

Once back inside, I scan the dance floor. No Ben. Tables? No Ben. Then I spot him, talking to an obviously distressed Valentina, in the corner near the dessert buffet.

Mmm. Dessert. But this is no time for distractions.

I take a deep breath, toss my fantastic (and still bouncy!) hair over my shoulder, and walk up to them.

Valentina looks like she's about to burst into tears. "Listen, Kelsey, I'm so, so—"

"Wait, wait, stop. There's no reason to be upset. I already knew—I mean, I didn't know about you, but . . . it's great. Really great. Seriously."

"Oh." She smiles. "Okay." Then she looks from me to Ben and smiles even bigger. "In that case . . . I'll go find JoJo. So . . . okay. Bye!"

"But Val, what about—," Ben calls after her. But she's gone. "Uh, hey, Kelsey. Hey. So, listen, I guess this is weird, or . . . I mean . . ."

I can't believe it. Where has the cocky newspaper guy gone? Ben looks positively *nervous*. Hm. Did Val tell him that I was talking to JoJo? Does he know that I know he likes me? Ahhh, it's not so fun when the shoe is on the other foot, eh, Mr. Photographer?

And just like that, I feel . . . totally, one hundred percent confident.

I say, "Hey, Ben. You want to dance with me?"

He looks relieved. "Yeah, okay. That'd be cool."

A slow song comes on (miracle!). Ben puts his arms around my waist and I'm actually touching him (!) and I put my head on his shoulder and he smells really nice. I see my friends dancing nearby and they all start making faces and winking at me like lunatics.

Very subtle, guys. Thanks.

"So . . . did you guys suddenly get a camera budget? For our poor, underfunded newspaper?" I ask, pulling my head back so I can look him in the eye.

He ducks his head, but I can see that he's blushing. "Well . . . no. I mean—"

"So you lied to me."

"I didn't *plan* to lie to you . . . I was just stalling until I found out what you were mad about. And then . . ."

"And then you found out I was mad at *you*, so you kept lying." I give him a stern look. This confidence thing is terrific!

"Seriously, look—the pictures were a total accident. Well, the last one was on purpose, but it was supposed to be a *good* pic. . . . Okay. I guess I really do need to pay more attention."

"Yeah, maybe blow up those thumbnails every once in a while. As someone who has been the victim of repeated, um, photographic assaults—"

"If only more enraged people complained, maybe the *Reflector* staff wouldn't be so lax. Maybe you should organize a group in your spare time. You know, when you aren't busy sabotaging plays and the like."

And . . . he's back. Crinkly eyes, the smile, the whole bit. *God, he is SO CUTE!*

"Yeah, good idea, thanks," I tell him. "I'll get right on that."

I put my head on his shoulder and try to relax. I mean, this isn't the time to be grouchy about *anything*. I'm dancing with Ben! At the prom! This is incredible!

Then one teeny, *tiny*, horrible thought creeps in. "Wait a second! Stop dancing!" I stop dancing. So does Ben.

"What's wrong?"

I peer at Ben suspiciously. "You aren't planning to put any pictures of me from the show in the paper, are you? In my costume, I mean? To be 'nice'? Or for any other reason?"

Ben grins, puts his hands back on my waist, and pulls me toward him again. "I guess you'll have to wait and see, Ms. Finkelstein. Either way, I bet you can handle it. Can't you?"

Yeah, probably, I think. I've definitely had plenty of practice in the dealing-with-abject-humiliation department.

I make a scowly face at him. Ben laughs, then gently tips my head onto his shoulder again. We sway to the music. And for the first time in maybe my entire life, my head isn't filled with a thousand thoughts about how this is unquestionably going to end in disaster. I'm not worried about impressing anyone, or saying the right thing, or looking a certain way, or anything. Actually, at the moment, I feel pretty psyched about just being plain old Kelsey Finkelstein.

It is really, really great.

I think I'd better confiscate that camera, though. Just to be on the safe side.